Snow Lane

Snow Lane

JOSIE ANGELINI

Feiwel and Friends
New York

A FEIWEL AND FRIENDS BOOK
An imprint of Macmillan Publishing Group, LLC
175 Fifth Avenue, New York, NY 10010

Our books may be purchased in bulk for promotional, educational, or
business use. Please contact your local bookseller or the Macmillan
Corporate and Premium Sales Department at (800) 221-7945 ext. 5442
or by e-mail at MacmillanSpecialMarkets@macmillan.com.

Library of Congress Cataloging-in-Publication Data

Names: Angelini, Josephine, author.
Title: Snow Lane / Josie Angelini.
Description: First edition. | New York : Feiwel and Friends, 2018. |
    Summary: In 1985 Massachusetts, fifth-grader Annie wants to
    shape her own future but as the youngest of nine, she is held back
    by her hand-me-down clothing, a crippling case of dyslexia, and
    a dark family secret. | Identifiers: LCCN 2017017594 (print) |
    LCCN 2017035722 (ebook) | ISBN 9781250150912 (EBook) |
    ISBN 9781250150929 (hardcover)
Subjects: | CYAC: Family life—Massachusetts—Fiction. | Schools—
    Fiction. | Friendship—Fiction. | Family problems—Fiction. |
    Dyslexia—Fiction. | Massachusetts—History—20th century—
    Fiction.
Classification: LCC PZ7.A58239 (ebook) | LCC PZ7.A58239
    Aah 2018 (print) | DDC [Fic]—dc23
LC record available at https://lccn.loc.gov/2017017594

Feiwel and Friends logo designed by Filomena Tuosto

First edition, 2018

1   3   5   7   9   10   8   6   4   2

mackids.com

For my daughter, Pia

Chapter One

My name is Antoinette Elizabeth Bianchi.

My name is longer than I am, or at least that's what my sisters say. Mostly, they call me Annie or Shrimpy, on account of the fact that I'm the youngest and the littlest and they're all super tall and they have tons of hair and big white teeth and they all talk with their hands a lot.

I'm not really small compared to other kids my age, it's just my sisters are larger than normal people. My eldest sister, Miriam, is only nineteen and she's been going to college for three years already because she skipped a grade. She's wicked smart. Miri does a lot of math—the kind that's all funny shapes and squiggly lines. I guess some people are so smart they don't need to use regular numbers like the rest of us.

I like my name, even if it was an accident. See, my mom was convinced I was going to be a boy and she wanted to name me Antony, but I came out a girl, so she just worked with what she had. My mom never throws anything away.

I live at 17 Snow Lane in Ashcroft, Massachusetts, I'm ten years old, and I'm the youngest of nine kids. I have seven big sisters and one big brother, which right now in 1985 is pretty rare, although my dad told me once that about a hundred years ago everyone had big families like we do. People often say that it must be so nice to have such a big family, and then they ask if it's fun to always have someone to play with.

I don't know what the hell (five Hail Marys) would give them that idea. Someone to play with? When you're the youngest of nine kids, you aren't a player. You're the ball.

My morning starts at six a.m. in midair. I don't mean I'm dreaming I'm flying. No, what I mean is that my sister Eleanor makes me sleep on the top bunk, even though I'm so skinny I sometimes slip between the mattress and the guardrail.

Our bunk bed is pushed up against the wall on one side. Our mom tells me to turn the other way when I go to sleep so I won't fall, but that doesn't help either. I end up sliding between the wall and the bed frame. Eleanor (she's the second youngest, and two whole years older than me; we call her Nora) has to yank on my arm and leg to get me unstuck, and I usually get wall-burn on the side of my face as she tugs. It actually sucks (five Hail Marys) more than just falling, so I don't sleep facing the wall anymore.

Our mom is just terrible at giving advice. Like throwing fire on gasoline. That's supposed to be the other way around, isn't it? Gas on a fire? I always get stuff like that mixed up. I'm dyslexic, my mom says, but my sister Fay says that's just a fancy way of saying I'm retarded.

Anyway, my mom doesn't give good advice, mostly because she doesn't listen. With nine kids she can hardly hear over all of us yelling, let alone listen to any one of us at a time, and I can understand that. But that doesn't make it easier. Because there are times I really need her to listen to me.

Like last year when I told her about ten times that my head was itchy and I probably had dandruff like in a TV commercial. She told me I didn't have dandruff without even checking me, and then the school nurse checked everyone in my school and it turned out I had lice, like, wicked bad. All my sisters and my brother were called out of classes and Aurora started crying on the car ride home and she said she'd never been so humiliated in all her life because now everyone thought we were dirty.

My mom doesn't really have much time for any of us kids. Miri told me once she wasn't always like that. Must've been nice.

I hit the ground with a whump.

"Ooh," I groan. The sound comes out creaky and uneven, like I'm a thousand years old. Nora squints at me from the bottom bunk.

"Hey, you landed on your back this time," she mumbles, still sleepy. "At least you won't have a black eye like last week."

"Uuummn," I wheeze. Something's wrong with my lungs. I can't seem to catch enough of a breath to do anything more than make weird noises. This is bad.

"Mom!" Nora yells, starting to worry about me. Normally, I would have picked myself up off the floor already, but for some reason I can't move.

Between the gray spots that are making everything fuzzy, I see my sister Virginia's face hanging next to Nora's above me. Virginia, who we call Gina, shares the room with us, even though she's fifteen and going to be a sophomore in high school when school starts up in a few weeks. Gina says she prefers rooming with us to rooming with Fay or Bridget, who are the next two down from her in age. I don't blame her. Fay and Bridget are mean. I'm glad I'm not stuck with them.

"Is she breathing?" Gina asks.

"Only kind of," Nora answers. She shifts from foot to foot anxiously. "Mom!" she calls out again, even though we all know it's useless.

Our mother isn't coming.

My sister Evangeline joins the upside-down circle of faces above mine. All their hair is dangling over me like ribbons in different shades of brown. Some curly, some straight. Gina's got a *ton* of split ends. She stopped doing her hair a few months ago when she got a pair of big shiny black boots and a ton of black T-shirts. She started wearing a lot of eyeliner, too. Most of my sisters wear eyeliner, except me and Nora. We aren't allowed to wear makeup or get our ears pierced yet. At twelve years old, Nora's almost old enough. I'm so jealous.

"Help me pick her up, Gina," Evangeline says urgently. Evangeline reaches for me, but Gina smacks her hands away.

"No, don't touch her!" Gina snaps.

Evangeline shakes out her precious hands, scowling at Gina. Evangeline's a pianist. She's only sixteen, but she's already played at Tanglewood (which is a place way the heck out in western Massachusetts, where people go to listen to fancy music outdoors). I like Tanglewood because you can run around while classical music is playing (which you totally can't do anywhere else), and even though the last time we went I got stung by a bee on my lip and Fay made fun of me, I didn't care because my dad bought me a sno-cone and sat next to me the whole time, which never happens because my dad works three jobs and never has time to sit down. I remember being there on the grass with my cherry sno-cone melting on my fat lip, the quiet shape of my dad, and how pretty Evangeline played.

"Pick her up," Evangeline orders in her serious voice. She's a year older than Gina, so that makes her the boss of the room right now.

The eldest is always the boss in my family. That means I'm not even the boss of the cat, Geronimo. He's older than my dad, practically, and I don't think anyone has ever tried to boss him about anything. I think about someone trying to boss that big old tomcat and start giggling. Or at least I try. I can't really laugh with no air.

"Why is she making that noise?" Nora asks.

Wow, it's like I'm thinking all these things and they're going so fast in my head, they just keep whooshing along, and things are starting to go a little dark around the edges. Maybe I should just go back to sleep.

"Don't move her! What if she's broken her neck?" Gina says, scowling.

I'm suddenly wide awake. Don't people with broken necks end up in wheelchairs? I saw this old movie once where a guy jumps into a pool but it's not filled up enough with water, so he hits his head on the bottom of the pool and almost drowns, and when he wakes up in the hospital he can't move and when the doctor comes in he says that it's because the guy broke his neck. I don't jump into pools now. Not that we have a pool or anything, because only rich people have pools.

It'd be nice to have a pool.

I try to wiggle something, but I can't tell if it works or not.

"Uuuunnng," I wheeze. I'm starting to feel really anxious, and there's nothing to count but sisters and I already know how many of them I've got. Counting calms me down when I'm nervous, even if they all call me Crazy when I do it.

"Oh no, oh no, oh no," Nora says. She's hopping around now and flapping her hands. "Mom!" she screams again. It looks like she's going to cry.

I don't know why, but if I see Nora crying I start to cry too, even if I'm not sad. Once Nora tried to shave her legs, but she did it wrong and she ended up cutting herself really bad and there was blood all over the sink (she tried to shave her legs in the sink, which I think was her big mistake), and when she saw the blood she started crying and then I started crying and Mom heard, so we got in so much trouble because we're not old enough to shave our legs yet, even though all the other girls Nora's age do it. Twelve-year-olds get to do everything. But we're Catholic, so we're not allowed to do much of anything. I look away from Nora so her crying doesn't get me started.

My sister Aurora glides into the room. She glides everywhere. She's a ballerina, but a real ballerina, not just someone who wants to be. She's part of the company at the Boston Ballet. She does *The Nutcracker* every winter, and I love it because I get to go backstage with her sometimes, and if the stage manager isn't looking, I can climb up into the rigging. It's so warm and secret up there. I love the smell of the ropes and the velvet curtains and the sound of the lights humming, and I love watching everyone dancing through the metal grating of the catwalk while I lie there facedown. Just floating over it all.

"What's going on?" Aurora says. She's seventeen, and the second eldest. She's only thirteen months younger than Miri, so that makes her boss of the room now.

"The baby fell," Gina says.

"Why did you leave her on the floor?" Aurora scolds. Gina drops her head and scowls, inching back. She mumbles something about a broken neck, but Aurora brushes it off like that's ridiculous. Aurora's good at waving a hand and making everyone else seem silly.

I can't see anything now except fuzzy gray shapes,

but I can smell Aurora's long black hair. Spicy and warm. She's so beautiful.

"She just got the wind knocked out of her. She'll catch her breath in a second," Aurora declares. "It's okay, Littlebit. Take slow breaths."

I love it when she calls me Littlebit. Way better than Shrimpy. And way, way better than my other nickname, Pukatrid, which is like puke and putrid put together.

Fay came up with Pukatrid when I went through what Mom called a "bad patch" when I was eight and I would puke over pretty much anything. And I mean *anything*. I'd puke if I ran too fast, or if my milk was a teensy bit too warm, but mostly I'd puke when someone was yelling, which someone always is around here. My mom said it was just because I have a delicate Constitution, but I don't know what puking has to do with John Hancock and all those guys in white wigs and silky pants. Or maybe that was the Declaration of Independence. I get them mixed up.

"Breathe slow and deep," Aurora says again, and she shows me how by doing it along with me.

It kind of works. I actually get some air in, and the lights turn on again.

"Nora, stop bouncing. Annie's going to be fine," Aurora says sharply. Nora's nerves annoy Aurora, which makes Nora extra nervous.

Nora goes and hides from Aurora behind Gina, because she's the biggest one in the room—she may not be the eldest, but Gina outweighs Aurora by, like, two Auroras.

It's not that Gina's fat. Well, not *really* fat. It's more like she's got better padding than the rest of us, but only because the rest of us would fit nice in a box of toothpicks. Except for my brother, JP, of course, but he's different because he's a boy. But Gina's got the prettiest skin and the bluest eyes. I wish I had eyes that blue. Mine are the color of pea soup, and no one's ever said pea soup was pretty.

Aurora scoops me up and smiles at me. Her face looks like a flower opening when she smiles. I put my head on her shoulder and wrap my legs around her waist like a monkey. She carries me into the hallway, and then downstairs to the kitchen. I can hear the dryer going in the basement. My mom is down there, doing laundry. I know she heard Nora calling her.

"How about a treat?" Aurora asks.

I shrug. I don't feel much like eating. I'm picturing my mom down in the basement, staring at the piles of clothes she's got to fold instead of coming upstairs to see what happened.

Aurora puts me down in a chair at our giant kitchen

table, which used to be a lab table at my dad's work. My dad's a chemist during the day, and at night he teaches math to grown-ups at the local college. On weekends he's a farmer, but mostly he's a chemist. He brought one of the lab tables home for us to use because a lab table is the only thing long enough to fit all ten of us (counting Miri when she's home) at dinnertime. I guess I should say eleven, including my dad, but he's always working. Usually I sit on the pew on the inside of the table. We call it the inside on account of the fact that you sometimes have to climb under the table to get to it, unless you're sitting on the end, like I always do.

I have to sit at the end next to my dad because he has to cut my meat for me. I'm not allowed to use steak knives after that one time I slipped and stabbed myself in the palm of my other hand. Went right through. Bled like crazy. Every time my heart beat, blood shot out, but we didn't go to the hospital or anything because my sister Fay managed to squeeze it hard enough to make it stop. That *really* hurt, but it stopped. I've still got the scar and it looks just like the hole Jesus has in his hand, but I'm not supposed to say that because that's blasphemy. I still think it, though, every day. My Jesus Hole.

My mom got the pew from the parish when they

were giving old stuff away, and she came home with a bunch of churchy things that are now all over the house and the yard. My mom's a church organist and my parents are super Catholic, so it makes sense that we have a statue of Saint Francis of Assisi in our bushes and a church pew in our kitchen.

All the little kids sit on the pew on the inside between the table and the wall because we don't need as much room as the bigger kids do. They sit in regular chairs on the outside, where I am now. It's weird to be on the outside of the kitchen table. I don't think I've ever sat here before.

Aurora opens the fridge and goes to her special drawer. She's the only one of us who has her own drawer, because she's got to take extra care of her figure, being a ballerina and all. If she has even one little pinch of fat over all that muscle she's got, she says she won't get good parts anymore, but personally, I think she's too skinny. Her food has to stay separate from our stuff so she knows exactly how much she's eaten, and the little kids aren't allowed to even look in there. She takes out a pomegranate. I know what it is because I asked her last time she was eating it, but she didn't give me any.

"Want to try?" she asks.

I nod again. I hold still so I don't wreck my chance

to finally taste it. Mom won't buy pomegranates for the rest of us kids because she says they're too expensive and wouldn't fill us up anyhow. Aurora peels open the rind and wiggles a section of juicy red seeds out of their white insides. I put them in my mouth and chew.

They taste exactly like I imagine rubies would taste. But better than the taste is knowing they're special.

"Good?" Aurora asks. I nod. "Now go upstairs and get changed."

I do what she tells me without even thinking of trying to get around it. When Aurora wants to be nice, she's the nicest. Especially to me. But when she's not feeling like being nice, you'd better watch out. She's like Mom that way.

Nora knows more about how scary Aurora can be than I do, though, because Aurora hates her. Which is weird, because when Nora was a baby, Aurora took care of her like Miri took care of me. All the older kids took care of us younger kids from Bridget down, because Miri told me by her fifth kid Mom couldn't do it anymore. I asked Miri why Mom kept having kids if she couldn't take care of us, and Miri said because we're Catholic. Catholics have to keep on having babies until God tells them they can stop or they go to hell.

There's a lot of ways to go to hell when you're Catholic, so I've spent a lot of time thinking about what it must be like. I've decided it must be like waiting for the bathroom in the morning.

There are only three bathrooms in our house. Mom and Dad have one in their room that we're not allowed to use, ever. The one downstairs is just for Aurora and Evangeline in the morning. It's only a sink and toilet, but it's enough room for the two of them to do their hair and makeup. The upstairs bathroom is the biggest. It has two sinks and a big mirror, a shower and a tub and a toilet, of course. This is the bathroom the rest of us use in the morning. My brother John Paul (JP for short) gets the big bathroom first, because he's fastest and he's the only boy. He also gets his own bedroom, but no one can really argue about that.

I pass JP on the stairs. "Hey, Annie," he says, smiling his big smile. JP always makes me happy. I smile back and try to squeeze past him, but I trip over about fifty things that are scattered up and down the sides of the steps. JP grabs my arm before I can tumble down the steps with the landslide of unopened mail and little figurines of angels and knitting patterns.

"Whoa! Watch out for Mom's stuff," he says, hauling me up by my arm. He ruffles my frizzy hair and gives me a little more space to get by. JP takes up a lot of room because he has a lot of muscles. He does a ton of sports at school and has, like, five letterman jackets, even

though he and Gina are both only going to be sopho-
mores when school starts up again.

Sometimes people call them Irish twins, but I don't
get it because most of the Irish people I know aren't
twins. Anyway, JP is like the exact opposite of Gina, so
maybe that's what they mean? Irish twins are like reverse
twins or something?

JP is super popular in school and good at pretty
much everything. You can't get into his bedroom without tripping over a trophy for sports or academics. Not
that I'm allowed in his bedroom, but still. I like that he's
always so nice to me and he always seems to listen when
I'm telling him how I'm upset about something. Maybe
that's why other people like him so much, too. JP does a
lot of listening, from what I can tell from all the girls
who are always hanging around him.

And Gina—well, Gina's not popular. She never gets
any phone calls, and she spends a lot of time listening to
this band called the Cure. For some reason that makes
her a big weirdo.

Now that JP's out of the bathroom, Virginia, Fay,
and Bridget dart in. Aw, crap (five Hail Marys). I missed
my one chance. Bridget slams the door in my and Nora's
faces.

"But I really have to go," Nora says, shifting from
foot to foot.

We hear the snap of a cassette tape as it's turned on. Music blares from behind the door. Led Zeppelin. "Whole Lotta Love."

"Please," Nora begs.

"You gotta sing the next line of the song," Fay yells back. The cassette is paused. I hear Bridget snickering.

"Yeah," Bridget says, because everything she says is something that Fay said first. "Sing the next verse of the song we were just playing and you can come in and pee."

"So childish," Gina says. "Just let her in."

"No!" Fay snaps back. "I want her to sing." When Fay gets an idea in her head, she'll die before she lets it go.

Nora's so full of pee her brown eyes are turning yellow, but I keep my mouth shut because if I say anything right now, Fay and Bridget will just get worse.

Nora doesn't have a choice. She clears her throat and tries to sing. "Way, way down inside—" She breaks off.

"And then?" Fay was laughing, but now she stops and she sounds totally serious. "There's more."

"It's just a bunch of yelling and noises," Nora says. She's crying now and I feel my throat choke up with her. It's like when the doctor hits your knee and your leg just shoots out. If Nora cries, I cry. "Come on, Fay, I can't hold it any longer!" she begs.

"Let her in," Virginia orders.

"No," Fay says. I can practically see the sneer on her lizard lips through the door. "Make me, *Vagina*."

Uh-oh.

Nora and I jump back as someone gets slammed into a wall on the other side of the door. There's a lot of snarling and slapping and their voices are really high and screechy. There's a thump as a body hits the floor.

It's even money, to tell you the truth. Gina's the biggest, but it's not like Fay is tiny like Nora and me. Fay has a thick back and really broad shoulders, like a boy. And she plays field hockey. She's like the captain or something, because she always finds a way to win.

Well, I know how she wins. She cheats. Fay cheats at everything, especially cards. Whenever we play, Fay always makes Nora give her the best cards, and if Nora doesn't, she hits her. Fay hits *hard*.

Bridget is having a conniption fit in there, she's laughing so hard. I hear them slam up against the door, and Nora and I jump back when we hear a splintering sound. Everything goes real quiet.

"Kids?" my mom calls.

I hear swearing on the other side of the door.

"What's going on up there?" my mom yells up the stairs. She comes to the bottom of the stairs, where she can see Nora and me standing outside the bathroom door. "What did you do?" she asks us. Just like my mom to show up only if there's something broken.

"Nothing," I say. "It was them in there."

My mom eyes Nora and sighs. "Go change your pants. Don't put those down the chute or the whole wash will smell like pee. Put them in the sink in my bathroom."

I look down and see Nora's wet herself. She's gone all pale and woozy like she does sometimes, and she's not moving even though I'm tugging on her.

"Come on," I say, grabbing her arm. I try to pull her into Mom and Dad's bedroom. "Quick, before Fay—" But she doesn't move fast enough.

"Before Fay what?" Fay asks as she pulls the bathroom door open.

"Nothing," I mumble, pushing Nora in front of me and trying to block the wet mark on the back of her pants.

Gina brushes past us and goes down the stairs and out the front door without even getting any breakfast. I glance back and see that the piece of plywood on the inside bottom part of the door has been all smooshed in.

See, our doors aren't like other people's doors. They're hollow inside, and they don't stand up to much. You could probably punch a hole right through with your forehead if you were standing too close when you sneezed.

"You two should be more careful," Fay says behind me. "I'm going to have to tell Mom what you did to the door."

"Hey," I say. "We didn't do that." Duh. Of course Fay knows we didn't do it. Don't know why I said that, except it was the first thing that popped into my head.

"Sure you did," Fay says. She crosses her arms. "Didn't they, Bridget?"

"I saw the whole thing," Bridget says, nodding and snickering.

I open my mouth to argue, and Fay leans forward and flicks me right on the Adam's apple. I can't think of anything to say after she does that. She and Bridget walk past us.

"Come on," I tell Nora, dragging her into the empty bathroom behind me. "I guess you'll have to wash off in the tub, too."

Her lips are all pressed together, and she's crying without making a sound. I've gotten good at that, too, but Nora's the champ. You'd never know she was crying if you didn't see the tears. Her shoulders don't even shake or anything.

"I hate her," she whispers after we've got her pants off and she's soaking in the tub.

Catholics aren't supposed to hate anybody except the devil. It's called Wrath, and it's one of the Seven Mortal Sins. I just nod because I don't want to say it and go to hell, but I'm thinking it. I'm also thinking it's so unfair that I'm not allowed to hate Fay when she really deserves it. God must have been an only child.

Chapter Two

Did I mention I grew up on a farm?

Well, technically, I don't *live* on the farm (that'd be awesome). My uncle Antonio and his wife, Constance, live on the farm. My uncle is older than my dad and he inherited most of it, and then we needed money (nobody would tell me for what) and my dad had to sell his part back to my uncle. All that happened before I was born, and now we just work the farm for extra money for our family. My aunt and uncle don't even have any kids. Why do they get all this space while the eleven of us are crammed into a tiny house on Snow Lane?

Being born first gives you lots of good stuff. Being born last, like my dad and me, means that everybody is your boss.

It's so hot on the farm in the summer, and there's no way to get out of the sun when you're working. Dad tells me to wear a hat, and I do, but it just feels hotter under it with no breeze, so I always end up taking it off.

And then I faint about half an hour later.

See, my dad's Italian, but my mom's Irish. Full red-headed Irish. All of my sisters got my dad's dark hair, and most of them got the kind of skin that gets pretty and golden in the sun, but not me. I just faint, burn, and then freckle.

So here it is. I'm skinny and shrimpy, with pouffy dishwater-blond hair (that's what Bridget calls it), and when I smile I look like a grand piano. People keep telling me I'll grow into my big teeth someday, but I don't know about that. I've got *giant* teeth. I have to concentrate to keep my lips shut. Fay tells me it makes me look dumber than I am to always have my mouth hanging open, but I can't be thinking about that all day or I'd never get anything done.

Having as many physical disadvantages as I do doesn't make me exempt from work, though. And today is a farm day, even though I'll be sore from falling out of bed this morning.

I go downstairs to the hall closet, where everybody's winter coats hang. At the bottom is the boot pile. The thing about the boot pile is that it's magic. Some days there's a pair that fits and then *bang*, the next day there's nothing. Sometimes you find just one stinking boot, and that's the worst because you can spend forever in the hall closet looking for something, but if it isn't your day, it isn't your day. And today's not my day.

"Annie, hurry up!" my mom shouts.

"I'm coming!" I holler back. I'll have to wear my sneakers, but I've already worn a hole in them and Mom says she won't buy me another pair yet because it's almost school shopping time. Not that I ever get anything new for school anyways.

I pull on my crummy sneakers and wiggle my big toe, looking at the hole. I'll have dirt and rocks in my shoe in under a minute, I bet. I run to the garage. Gina is up front with Mom. Fay, Bridget, and Nora are already in the back of the van. JP is probably at his Youth Fellowship meeting with the monks, and Evangeline and Aurora are on the T to Boston to rehearse with the symphony and the ballet. I climb into the back.

"Did you tinkle?" Mom asks. I climb out of the van and run back upstairs to tinkle.

When I come back down, my sisters are all looking at me like I'm something they stepped in. It's a long drive, and nobody likes being in the van for one second longer than they have to because the van is the van.

There are some cars, like the blue Chevy Nova,

which used to belong to my aunt Mary Perpetua (she gave it to Miri when Miri went to MIT), that are difficult and smelly like the van is, but you still like to ride in them because they have something about them that's easy to love. The van is the most unlovable car ever made. It has no seats in the back (there are only two seats up front, one for the driver and one for the person lucky enough to ride up there, which is never me). There is no padding of any kind in the back of the van, and no straps to hang on to when the driver takes a sharp turn. And the air vents don't have filters, so it always smells stinky, like car exhaust. Going to the farm in the back of the van is like spending an hour in a dryer with a bag of rocks and a fart.

"You put your shirt on backwards," Bridget says.

"Darn," I reply, looking down and realizing she's right.

The thing about being dyslexic is that you think things are all lined up and doing exactly what they should, but there's a difference between looking at something and how it's going to look on you. I know that, but I can't see it. My mom used to lay my clothes down on the floor for me just like I was supposed to wear them. I'd lie on top of them and then wiggle in. Easy peasy. But she stopped laying out my clothes a few months back because I'm supposed to be old enough now. I don't know what old enough has to do with it. Unless she means that I'll grow out of being dyslexic someday. I hope so.

I pull my arms inside my T-shirt, spin it around, and stick my arms out through the holes again.

"It's still inside out," Bridget tells me.

I go to pull my shirt off over my head to flip it and Fay yells at me.

"No, don't take your clothes off! People can see in the windows," she says, pulling my shirt back down over my head. "God, why can't you learn how to dress yourself? I'm sick of doing it for you."

"She isn't even wearing a bra," Bridget says, like I'm some kind of freak. But I don't need a bra yet. There's nothing there to put in one.

I can't think of a time Fay has ever dressed me, but it doesn't matter. Everyone's so frustrated with me I start to feel anxious again. I look for something to count but there are no other cars yet, so no other license plates.

As my mom steps on it to merge onto the freeway, we tumble across the bumpy iron floor of the van.

Nora catches me and shows me which way is up as my mom cuts the wheel to change lanes. I brace myself against the wall and smile at her for saving me some bruises. I see Fay and Bridget shaking their heads at me.

"Retard," Fay whispers. She looks away like she can't stand to see me anymore.

I look out the window and watch the dark green leaves of the summer trees flick by, but it's only so I don't start counting. Nora doesn't mind when I do it, but Fay, Bridget, and Gina hate it because they say it makes them look weird by relation and I'm already in enough hot water with everyone for not peeing before I came down and I don't want to get a slap. I keep my eyes glued to the leaves, trying to ignore the license plate numbers and the mile marker numbers and the exit numbers.

I try to tell myself not to start adding, and not to start putting the sums together into multiples of three and then take the threes and put them in sets of threes, and count the sets. But I can't help it. I see numbers coming together and branching out all the time when they fly by me like they do on the Mass Pike. It makes me feel calm. Crap (five Hail Marys), I need a two to fix that seven so I have a nine to round out my eighteenth set. I hold the four on the back of the Volvo in a "remainder set" while I search for a two or a five or an eight—

"Your lips are moving," Nora whispers in my ear. She slides in front of me and hands me a comb. "Braid my hair," she tells me.

I sigh and gratefully start sectioning her hair into threes. Now I can count for a reason. I'll do three rows of French braids. Nora's hair is slippery-soft and she's got a ton of it, so I'll have to pull it tight. I'll be at it for-ever, which is a good thing.

I don't mind Shrimpy. I don't mind Pukatrid. But I hate to be called Crazy. It's how they look at me when they say it that bothers me. Like they're worried about me. Or maybe they're scared. Miri told me once that I was wicked smart like her, and that's why people are afraid of me when I do stuff with numbers they don't under-stand. I loved that she said that. I loved it most that she said we were alike. But I don't really get what she means when she says I'm smart like her. Miri's got to be way smarter than me, because Fay and Bridget always say I'm an idiot.

You'd think since I like counting so much I'd be great at math, but I'm not. It's the shape of the numbers that I like to think about. How they fit together. It's making a rule, like, I'm going to add the numbers on a license plate as it flashes past. If the numbers add up to a multiple of, say, three, five, or seven, then that's the rule today. I look at another license plate as it flashes by and add the numbers on it. If they don't add up to a mul-tiple of five, I have to keep adding new sets of license plate sums until I get a sum that is divisible by five. Then I start over.

Today it was multiples of three, which also happens to be my favorite. I add up the numbers as they go by, and if I can get the plates from three cars to add up to a number divisible by three (and nine is my favorite, because *duh*), then it fits the rule for today. And when I get the numbers to fit, I feel better. Like, something you can't prepare for—a license plate flashing by—adds up just the way you want it to and that means that everything is going to be okay today. Sometimes it means I have to hold dozens of numbers in my head to make the sets work, but that's easy for me. I can remember long strings of numbers without any trouble at all. I'm good at it. Being good at it makes me feel calm. It's like I don't even need to think because I'm thinking so hard. I can't really explain it, but sometimes it's a pain because I can't shut it off. Especially on days when I'm nervous.

I didn't find the damn (ten Hail Marys) two I needed. But now I braid it into Nora's hair. I'll do three sets of three strands of hair and I'll only use two rubber bands to tie it off. Shazam. I've got my two.

Honestly, I don't know why my sisters think my counting is so weird. Our mom has about a half-dozen rosary beads hanging from the rearview mirror, and when she's stuck in traffic, she takes one down and starts counting prayers on it. Mom whispers her Hail Marys and her Glory Be's from the front seat. Why is me whispering license plate numbers that much different? But everyone in my family is worried about how things look to other people.

When we finally get to the farm, I'm carsick from staring at the back of Nora's head. I get out of the van and brace my hands on my knees, looking at the ground real hard. I take a deep, cool breath. The best part about the farm is the ocean breezes. We're not too far from the coast, and every now and again you get a tangy, salty sort of breeze that's about ten degrees cooler for about five seconds before it goes back to being ninety degrees out again. But for that five seconds, it's really nice.

What sucks (five Hail Marys) about it is knowing that I'm so close to the ocean but I haven't been to the beach all summer, and I probably won't go there once this year because Mom says I'm not allowed to swim anyway on account of the fact that I always seem to aim right for a riptide.

"She's gonna barf," Gina warns, holding Bridget back so she's out of the blast zone.

"No, I'm n—" I say, and then barf comes shooting out of me. Ugh. I wasn't ready for it, so most of it comes out my nose. Now I'll smell barf all day. Wait, did I eat something blue?

I hear my sisters groaning. Calling me gross.

"I can't help it," I say, still bending over in case there's more. Yup. There's more.

Another chunky rainbow splats out of me. This one sounds like I'm shouting for some guy named Hughie, which makes me laugh, which is disgusting because I suck a ton of puke back up my nose and re-swallow it, which makes me barf again. And now I'm trapped in the never-ending barf cycle, where your barf grosses you out so much all you can do is barf more. At this point, I think I might actually barf forever.

"She's really going at it today," Gina says. "Just try to calm down, Shrimpy," she tells me. She rubs my back and it feels nice. "Calm down and you'll stop. It's okay."

She keeps rubbing and I start to feel better. I spit a few times and stand up, finally out of the barf cycle.

"Got a tissue?" I ask.

Nora goes into the front seat of the van and raids Mom's tissue stash. Mom's got tissues stored all over the place. Can't go five feet in our house without coming across a box of tissues. In the winter, Mom even keeps a tissue balled up in her sleeve, just in case.

I blow my nose while Nora gets the hose and runs some water over my puddle of yuck.

"Maybe a flower will grow here," Nora says with a little smile on her face. I haven't seen her smile in a long time.

"Yeah." I laugh. "I just hope it doesn't look like what it came from."

"The barf blossom."

"We'll give it to Aunt Constance."

She and I grin at each other and she hands me the hose. I rinse out my mouth and wash my face.

The water on the farm is so good. It's well water. Cold, cold, cold, like it's always winter underground, and sweet like it's never touched a metal pipe. I could drink buckets of it.

Nora turns off the hose and we go into the mudroom under the farmhouse. We're not allowed inside the house. Aunt Constance doesn't like us stomping on her clean floors with our dirty boots. Aunt Constance doesn't like us, period.

The walk to the mudroom is enough to fill my holey sneaker with pebbles. Nora lifts the rusty latch and swings open the door. It makes a low hooting noise, almost like a *helloooo*. I like that sound. I also like the smell of the mudroom. It smells exactly like you'd think a mudroom would smell. Like clay and dusty wood.

It's dark in the mudroom. Dark and cold. It never gets warm down here no matter how hot it gets outside. It's like the well water. On the farm, winter is always waiting, just a few inches down.

There are two windows, but I wouldn't really call them windows. They're just little portholes at opposite ends of the mudroom, always clogged with spiderwebs, but they let in a tiny bit of light. There's a bathroom, too. Well—how do I describe the bathroom down here? You have to duck. You have to squat. You have to aim. And you have to hope nothing with more legs than you decides to bite you when your pants are down.

The mudroom also has another room at the back. But I don't go there. It smells like blood.

I sit down on the dusty steps just inside the door, take off my sneaker, and shake out my pebble passengers. My father, who was up at the farm an hour before us because he's got so much work to do, is already handing out jobs.

My dad isn't really a farmer. Or he isn't really a chemist. Actually, I don't know which he isn't, because he's both.

Everyone starts stepping over me to get out to the fields while I'm holding my shoe in my hand. I hop over to my dad.

"Wait, where am I going again?" I ask him.

He looks at me and wrinkles his already permanently wrinkled forehead. We have the same green eyes. I notice it when he looks at me like he is now, but he doesn't look at me very much.

"Well," he says quietly, "what do you want to do?"

My dad is always quiet. The only time I've ever heard

him raise his voice is when he's shouting over the noise of the tractor.

"Well," I reply. "What do you need me to do?"

I want to be helpful. I want to be one of his strong daughters, like Fay or Gina. Fay and Gina always get the important jobs. But Fay and Gina can also both bench-press twice their weight, and our dad knows it. He looks me over. I know he can see I'm still a little pale and shaky from the knock I took when I fell out of bed, and from barfing when I got out of the van. I'm good at counting, and so is my dad. We have the same eyes, so I see things like he does.

"We have a few orders for blueberries. Why don't you get a basket and go with Eleanor?"

Blueberries are the easiest. No thorns, like the raspberries. No crouching, like the strawberries. No heavy lifting, like the tomatoes. And the bushes are old enough and tall enough that you're always in the shade when you're picking.

Dad's giving me the lightweight job. Again. And I'm not even in charge of the blueberries. Nora is.

He gives me a weird look. "Your shirt's on inside out," he tells me.

I look down at my shirt and open my mouth. I know I have something to say, but it doesn't come out in time.

My dad is already stomping up the three steps out of the dark mudroom and into the blazing light of the fields before I can tell him that of course I knew that. It's a fashion choice. Why does the perfect thing to say always come to me way after it makes any sense for me to say it?

May as well get to work. I jump up to knock free one of the ancient woven wicker baskets that hang on pegs from the thick wooden beams that support the ceiling of the mudroom. I catch my basket as it and I fall back to the ground.

I like picking blueberries. I tie the basket around my waist with a bandanna and go out into the sun. I whistle a little bit and swing my arms, setting the mood. Today didn't start out that great, but it's still early. I can turn this around.

I walk out into the tall grass between the farmhouse and the old blueberry bushes and get soaked with dew up to the thigh. That'll keep me cool. It'll also make me itchy in about two seconds, but what can you do? It's hot or itchy on the farm, and on most days it's both.

Nora is already out here somewhere, but I can't see her because the bushes are huge. They were my nonna's. My nonno planted them for her when she first came to America because blueberries were her favorite. That makes them older than Dad, and there isn't much left in the world older than him, or at least that's what my sisters say.

I tuck myself into a bush with lots of ripe berries on it and start to pick. Blueberry bushes have smooth, glossy leaves with no irritating hairs on them, so you can get right inside the cool branches while you pick and be out of the sun. It's easy work, but after just a few minutes it's dead boring. Good thing I've never had a watch or I'd always be checking it.

The one thing that I like about picking berries is it gives me plenty of time to think about whatever I want to think about. Mostly I think about what it would be like to be anybody but me. I think about what it would be like to have superpowers. Or what it would be like to live back when there were knights and dragons. I'd have liked to have been a knight and swing a sword and say *forsooth*. Nora says that girls can't be knights, but I've figured out a way around that. I'd just cut my hair and pretend to be a boy. No one would notice on account of the fact that I'm flat as a board. I'd totally fight dragons. Nora says there's no such thing as dragons, but how would she know? She wasn't alive back then.

Nora also says I can't use the Force because there's no such thing. My mom said the Force is witchcraft anyhow and all the Jedi are going to hell. That doesn't make any sense. The Jedi are good. Good people don't go to hell, I said, but my mom said that anyone who uses witch-craft can't be good, even if they do good things. I guess it doesn't matter what you do, just as long as you aren't a witch.

I'd have liked to have been a witch and cast spells and flown around on a broomstick and been super-powerful, but I'd never tell my mother that or I'd spend the rest of my life getting lectured by some priest. I don't like priests. They're creepy, but I'm not supposed to say that out loud.

I hear Nora coming toward me and stick my head out of the bush.

"How much do you have?" she asks. She looks in my basket and then back up at me. She isn't happy. "That's it?" she asks. "That's all you got in three hours?"

I look in her basket. She's got, like, five times as much as me. "No way! How'd you pick that much?"

She rolls her eyes. "Come on. Let's measure it out and hope we got enough, because Dad wants us to move to raspberries now."

"Why?" I ask, struggling to keep up with her. Her legs are longer than mine.

"Because they're ready and we have to pick them today or we lose a lot of money," she answers, kind of yelling.

"Why are you so mad at me?" I ask. "Why is everyone so mad at me today?" Nora sighs a lot when I do stuff that bugs her, but she doesn't really get mad at me that often. Her lips are all pressed together, and I think for a second she's not going to answer me, but she finally does.

"You need to start pulling your weight, Annie. Whenever you don't pick enough or"—she gestures to my T-shirt—"dress yourself right, that means one of us has to do it for you, because Mom and Dad can't."

She said *can't*, but I know her better than anybody. The way she said it, like she's sad, sounds like she means *won't*. She shakes her head, sorry that she snapped at me. Nora and I almost never yell at each other.

"You have to grow up faster and look after yourself like the rest of us did, even if you are only ten. You can't be a kid anymore, because no one wants to take care of you."

I nod because I know all this, but it still makes me feel stupid to hear it. Then Nora gives me a little sideways hug and it cheers me up.

"Now hurry up," she says, heading back toward the farmhouse. She's smiling a little when she says it, and if Nora smiles, I smile.

"I'm coming," I say, huffing along. Woo, it got hot. I wipe my upper lip and blink the sweat out of my eyes.

We go back into the mudroom and dump our

blueberries into pint baskets. I got four measly pints. Nora got nine, but we need eighteen. I look over at the filled flats of raspberries. A flat has twenty-four pints in it. Gina and Fay must be picking their brains out today. They've got three full flats between the two of them.

Okay, so Bridget is out there with them, but Bridget is even slower at picking than I am, because she doesn't even try. She just stands around worrying about her tan line, although I don't know why she cares so much about getting a crooked tan. A straight tan isn't going to help. I always wonder how someone as plain as Bridget got to be so concerned about how she looks. No one's ever called me beautiful, but Aurora says Bridget looks like she was put together with construction paper and a stapler and she's still always got her face pressed against a mirror.

"You go back to the blueberries, and I'll go help Gina," Nora says with a sigh.

It's almost noon and blazing hot right now. "No, I'll go," I tell her. I'm going to prove to her I can take care of myself. "You finish up with the blueberries, and I'll help them because I was so slow."

I don't let her argue with me; I just set up some pints in a carry flat. Raspberries are so fragile you have to pick them and place them directly into a pint basket or they turn to jam on you. Our mom calls them *persnickety*, but

I don't know if that's a real word or not, so I don't use it anyplace but in my head. I sit down on the step, untie my shoe, and shake a ton of rocks out. At this point I've got more dirt in my shoe than outside of it.

I put my dirty sneaker back on and go out into the sun. I feel my skin pucker with sweat just like my mouth does when I lick something sour. I wonder if drool and sweat are the same thing. I laugh as I head out to the raspberries, thinking of my skin drooling.

My sisters look up from the raspberry canes like I've got three heads. Fay rolls her eyes. I stop laughing. Gina looks hassled, and she points me to the end of her row.

"Pick toward me," she tells me.

I trudge to the end of the row (gathering up a ton of dirt and rocks in my leaky shoe on the way), bend down a bit, and stick my hands in between the thorns.

The first raspberry is for me. I squish it around my mouth. I like the seeds. I like how they taste kind of oily inside the sweet and sour of the berry. I pop the seeds between my teeth as I tug more ripe berries into my hand. I love the taste of raspberries, but they are the meanest things to pick. Even the leaves have tiny little thorns on the edges and on the underside. The real kicker is that the thorns have a bit of venom on them. Just a bitty scratch and your skin swells up, and if your hand gets too full of berries, your fist will be too big to take out of the bush without getting scratched to king-dom come.

If you want to eat raspberries, then you have to let them eat you a little bit, too.

It's hot. There's no shade, no wind, no birds, and even the insects have packed it in. It's so hot and quiet I think I can almost hear the sun coming in waves. In no time my forearms are all scratched up and stinging with sweat. I want to rub the scratches, but that will only make them sting more. I look down at my pint baskets, and only two are filled.

Why am I so slow?

"Annie?"

I try to be careful. I try to focus. I was picking as fast as I could, and then I started thinking about how the sun sounded and how me and the raspberries are eating each other, and . . .

"She's fainting!" Gina yells.

I giggle because I can't see anyone fainting. All I can see is the sky. It's beautiful.

Chapter Three

It's the first day of school.

I know I should be more excited. I like school. I have lots of people to talk to and the teachers are nice and I'm almost always the first kid to understand what the heck is going on when we learn a new lesson.

I'm good at school.

Well, except for spelling. When I put the letters down they look okay to me, and to be fair, I almost always have all the right letters. I'm just usually wrong about the order they're supposed to go in. But I'm an ace at understanding what I read as soon as I get the letters to stop crawling all over the dang page, so apart from the occasional spelling test, I get all As without trying. I just listen in class and I know all the answers without having to study, 'cause things tend to stick in my head even if I don't want them to.

You'd be surprised what gets stuck in my head. TV jingles and the price of tuna fish and just about everything there is to know about Dwight D. Eisenhower. I had to do a report on him last year. Operation Overlord was the code name for when they stormed the beaches of Normandy. I like the word *overlord*. I keep looking for a place to use it, but it hasn't come up yet, so the word just rattles around in my head, waiting for the chance to get said. I guess my brain is like my mom. It doesn't ever throw anything away either.

I like school, but this year I'm not excited for the first day because of my destroyed sneakers. Mom said they'd make it a few more weeks, until it turns cold. I didn't get any new clothes, either. I didn't fit any of Nora's hand-me-downs. They're too loose around the waist or not long enough in the leg, and most of her shirts were already hand-me-downs from, like, three other people, so they're worn so thin you could throw a cat through them and Mom said it wasn't decent for me to wear them until I get my first bra. Which will be never, considering what I'm working with. Ribs and skin. My chest looks like a xylophone with two pinkish moles on it. The only clothes that fit me are JP's Sunday button-downs and his old jeans, and I don't want to wear boy clothes, seeing as how I look so much like a boy as it is.

It's not just that they're boy clothes. It's that they're boy clothes from ten years ago. I don't think any of the other girls at my school are going to be wearing button-down shirts, beat-up old sneakers, and bell-bottom jeans. I look in the mirror and take my hair out of my usual low ponytail so I look a little more like a girl. It doesn't really help. I don't look like other girls, and I never have, to be honest.

I don't know what to do.

I try to wash my sneakers. I take them to the sink and wet an old rag, but the dust just turns to mud. I'll have to rinse them off. Maybe I should use some soap.

"What are you doing?" Nora asks. She comes in and turns off the tap.

"I'm trying to clean off some of the dirt," I say. I'm starting to panic now because I realize my sneakers are still filthy, and now they're soaked, too.

"Annie, we have to go. The bus is coming," she tells me.

I sit down on the floor and pull on my wet sneakers. My face feels hot.

"You think anyone will notice?" I ask. When I stand up, I make a squelching sound.

Nora sighs. "Come on," she says, but she isn't angry

or anything. "We'll sit at the front of the bus so you don't have to walk by anyone."

My shoes go *squish, squish, squish* all the way out the door. At least I don't have to stand at the bus stop with anyone but Nora, because everyone else on our block is in high school and Nora and I are the only ones still in middle. I'm in fifth grade this year and she's in seventh, and Fay is in eighth and Bridget is in ninth. Eighth and ninth grades are in the high school in my town for some dumb reason. I look into the woods across the street as I jump up and down, trying to stamp the water out while we wait for the bus. It doesn't work. All it does is make the hole in the toe even bigger. Nora crosses her arms and shakes her head.

"You're just making it worse," she says, her voice kind of sad, kind of tired.

She looks away like we're not together as the bus pulls up. I sit down next to her in the first seat without looking up, because I don't want anyone to notice me. The hole in my sneaker and my boys' clothes bother me, and I don't know why. My clothes and shoes didn't used to be a big deal to me, unless they were uncomfortable. I've never had anything new, but just this once I wish I had new sneakers for the first day back at school.

"Hi, Annie! Did you have a good summer?"

I look up and see Kristin Gates standing over me.

"Yeah!" I say, even though I spent half the summer working on the farm, fainting or barfing. "How was your summer?" I ask.

Kristin sits down in the seat across the aisle from Nora and me. She's in my grade and she lives just down the hill from us. I like Kristin. She's smart and she has super-straight blond hair and one dark freckle on her left cheek that looks like an itty-bitty star.

I glance down at her shoes while she sits. She's wearing bright white sneakers, and her socks are pale pink and scrunchy. Everything she's wearing reminds me of cotton candy. Kristin is an only child. Her house is so quiet and her clothes are always new. I look back up at her, but she isn't looking at my shoes like I'm looking at hers. She's looking right at me and she's smiling. Kristin is always smiling.

"It was amazing," she says.

"Yeah?" I say, feeling her smile make me smile.

"I went to camp. It was so fun. We went hiking and berry picking." Kristin breaks off and reaches into her brand-new backpack, not catching my frown. Why does everyone talk about berry picking like it's awesome? "And we learned how to make friendship bracelets," she says. "Hold out your hand."

I hold out my hand and she puts something in it. I open my palm and see she's given me a purple-and-green woven thing. I look up at her, confused.

"That's a friendship bracelet," she says. She laughs and shows me her wrist. It has five of these brightly colored woven bracelets around it. And it looks so *cool*.

"I love it," I say, not sure what to do. "How do I put it on?" Kristin shows me how to tie it so the ends lie flat. "You made this for me?" I ask.

"Yeah," she says, rolling her eyes a little. "And now you can't make a friendship bracelet that's purple and green for anyone but me, because those are our colors."

"Okay," I say, nodding frantically. "Purple and green. You and me."

"You're so funny, Annie," she tells me. "I missed you."

"I missed you, too," I say. I realize after I say it that I mean it. It's so fun to smile and let your voice rise up high, almost like you're singing half your words. We don't talk like that in my house. "So, tell me about camp."

While my sister stares out the window, ignoring us, what I learn is that camp is a magical place. It's full of songs and swimming and big shady trees. Camp is where you make friendship bracelets and spend the day floating along in a canoe and eating something called s'mores. It has marshmallows in it. Kristin can't believe I've never eaten a marshmallow, but it's true. We can't afford to eat store-bought sweets in my family, but I skip over that and beg Kristin to keep talking. I want camp. I want to live there someday.

"You should come with me next year," she tells me as the bus pulls up the drive to school. "You'd really love it, Annie. And everyone would love you because you're so easy to talk to."

"Maybe you're just easy to listen to," I tell her instead of telling her the truth: I'll never go to camp. She smiles so wide I can see every one of her teeth.

"That's why I love you, Annie."

I smile at her. Kristin says she loves people all the time, and I like that about her, because it makes me think she could probably love the whole world if she put her mind to it. It makes me happy to think that—that there's a person who's so nice they could love everybody. I try to be like that, but most days I can't.

When we get off the bus, she loops her arm in mine and we go like that to homeroom, our arms linked together like we're on our way to eat marshmallows in a canoe. I'm about two feet taller than her and I have to stoop down so I don't elbow her in the lip, but I'm laughing and skipping along with her anyways, because it feels nice to be one of those girls who laughs and skips.

We both have Mrs. Weiss for homeroom because

Kristin and I are in a special class together. It's called ACT, which is short for Academically Creative and Talented. Kristin is the smartest girl in our grade, so she totally belongs in ACT.

I'm in ACT because I took this weird test when I was seven and it was all puzzles and questions about what groups I would make out of a bunch of odd shapes.

The people who tested me kept giving me funny looks when I'd answer, but they were nice and they let me answer out loud rather than write it down. I like figuring things out in my head rather than writing them down, because whenever I write things down, the letters and numbers start to wiggle all over the page.

I thought I did okay. But then afterward all the adults stood around looking at me and frowning and talking about *what needed to be done* about me like I was sick or something. And then they put me in ACT, which I thought was a mistake because Fay always says I'm stupid. Miri thinks I'm smart, though, and Miri's *waaay* smarter than Fay.

I like ACT because all I have to do is think about what I want to think about and tell the class about it later. They're called oral dissertations, which means you do them out loud, but sometimes I get to use models, like the time I wanted to think about DNA because I was wondering why I was the only one in my family who got my dad's green eyes.

I did about a jillion Punnett squares but it didn't add up, so my dad and I built a double helix out of a bunch of painted wood blocks so I could see how easy it is for the nucleotides to get scrambled sometimes during the unzipping, and if even a few nucleotide pairs get scrambled, you get a different gene. Green eyes means your DNA is scrambled between brown and blue. I get that now because of the model, and it makes sense to me because I've always felt a little scrambled in how I see things. But mostly it was fun because everyone really liked the color I picked for adenine. Hot pink.

Kristin painted her fingernails almost the exact same shade for a month afterward. I always think of nucleotides when I see hot pink now, which is good and bad. It's good because it makes me smile, but it's bad because I can't tell anyone else why I'm smiling without sounding like a freak. There are times when I think that no one in the world is ever going to understand what makes me smile, and I probably shouldn't try to explain it to anyone, because there are some things that are just never going to make sense to other people.

There are eight of us in ACT and everyone is, like, way smarter than me. We still have all the regular classes the other kids do, we just do ACT as extra. Everyone else in ACT gets 100s on everything in the other classes, including spelling. But I'm glad I'm there even if it is extra, because I get to think my own things and I don't have to turn in a project until I've figured out whatever it is I'm thinking about, like with my green eyes. Basically, the teachers leave me alone.

We get to homeroom and Mrs. Weiss already has something written on the blackboard.

We are star stuff which has taken its destiny into its own hands.

—Carl Sagan

WHAT IS YOUR DESTINY?

It takes me a few seconds to untangle the letter salad on the blackboard, but eventually I manage to make all the vowels behave long enough to get it.

And it's like I'm standing on top of a hill, looking down at the whole world.

A couple of years ago my dad let us watch this special on PBS. Normally we don't get to watch TV because the Solid Gold Dancers are pornographic, but my dad made an exception for Carl Sagan, probably because he doesn't do any dancing at all on his show *Cosmos*.

I wished I could have watched that show forever, because every time he said "billions and billions," I felt like I was as small as a nucleotide but just as important. I felt like I was a part of something that's bigger than I can see, bigger than any of us can see, and that's the best part. Every time Carl Sagan pointed out how little we all are, no one was bigger than me. No one was more important. Infinity makes us all equal somehow. I like that.

And now Carl Sagan wants me to find my destiny.

This is important. This is something that's really going to make everything okay, even better than finding a license plate with three threes. I'm going to find my destiny, and then it will all make sense because even when you're scared, having a destiny means you're going to be okay, because people with destinies don't just shit (fifteen Hail Marys) the bed.

I'm not supposed to swear even in my own head, but sometimes you need a word with a little more oomph in it than a regular word, so a swear word is the only thing that will work. This is a swear-word moment. This is the moment I'm going to find my destiny.

Crap (five Hail Marys). What the heck is my destiny?

"Annie? Would you take your seat, please?"

I look down at Mrs. Weiss. She's about two inches shorter than me, which is weird because she's my teacher, but I'm getting used to adults being littler than me because all the Bianchis are taller than normal people.

I take a seat next to Kristin and behind Jordan Dolan. If Kristin is the smartest person in our class, Jordan isn't far behind. He's quiet, but when he says something, I like to listen, because he hardly ever says anything that doesn't mean twice as much in half the words.

Jordan turns around and smiles at me. "Hi, Annie," he says.

"Hi, Jordan," I say back. "You're tan."

He nods and purses his lips like he's thinking of what to say next, but he decides against talking for a while. Jordan does this a lot. I'm used to it because my dad is the same way. When my dad is actually around, he hardly gets a word in edgewise what with all of us jabbering at him day and night. I wonder how Jordan got to be like he is, seeing as how he doesn't have eight daughters who are all as chatty as a flock of seagulls. Jordan does have a lawyer mom, though. Maybe that's it.

Anyways, I can tell he's got a lot to say, but I know from being around my dad that if I even take a breath to talk, he'll clam up and I'll never know how he got his tan. I sit still and wait even though it's, like, torture.

"I built a boat," he tells me after being quiet for a long while.

I'm trying to picture that, but I can't. I need scale. "Do people fit in it?" I ask.

He nods.

"Does it float with people in it?" I ask, still trying to picture Jordan's boat.

He nods again.

I glance down at his hands, and I can see how they got square and rough as compared to last year. I know what his hands look like really well, because Jordan and I always get paired up for stuff, mostly because he picks me as a partner. Probably because I don't rush him when he's deciding which five or six words are worth saying. I think Jordan's hands are bigger than mine now, which is strange.

He takes a breath like he's going to ask me something, but he never gets the chance. The bell rings and Mrs. Weiss stands in front of the blackboard.

I like teachers. I know that's a goody-two-shoes thing to say, but it's true. I always nod when the teacher asks a question you're supposed to answer yes to, and I always laugh when they've told a joke that isn't all that funny, because I get so uncomfortable when they're looking for something and no one is giving it back to them. My teachers try really hard, and most people don't try hard at anything.

"Hello, fifth graders. Welcome!" Mrs. Weiss says with way too much enthusiasm.

I smile big for Mrs. Weiss, and not just because I'm embarrassed for her for trying too hard. Some teachers are like that. They try too hard to be cool and peppy. I'm always nice to those teachers, though, because at least they try. I like Mrs. Weiss.

"You've all had a chance to read what I wrote on the blackboard, correct?" she asks, already knowing the answer. "Who here knows who Carl Sagan is?"

Every hand goes up. Jordan even laughs a little, like he's saying, *Of course we know who he is.*

It's weird to think Jordan and Kristin might have been watching the same TV program I was watching, and maybe even at the same time.

I look over at Kristin's T-shirt. It has a cat on it and the whiskers are sparkly with glitter. Her jeans are the palest shade of blue. I look at Jordan with his polo shirt, khakis, and Docksiders. His socks are so white and his hair is freshly cut. I can see a pale strip of skin on the back of his neck.

I imagine Kristin and Jordan watching Carl Sagan at the exact same moment as me. I see them in pajamas. I see them on big couches. I see them eating snacks, because rich people have pajamas and big couches and snacks. I bet they weren't a little bit hungry while they watched.

I bet they could hear every word because there was no yelling, nobody started hitting anybody else, and no one ended up going to bed scared. Just because you see the same TV show doesn't mean you saw it the same way.

"This year for ACT, I want you all to start thinking about your own individual talents," Mrs. Weiss says. I can tell she's being extra serious because her eyebrows are all squished together and it looks like she's going to cry. "I want you to think about what your unique talent could mean to the world if you applied it to a profession."

Jimmy Collins raises his skinny arm. All of Jimmy Collins is little and skinny, except for his ears. You don't normally think of ears as fat, but there's no other way to put it. Jimmy Collins has fat ears. It's not just that they stick out, it's that they're big and fleshy like ears aren't supposed to be. His earlobes are thicker than thumbs. He gets teased a lot, but not by anyone in ACT.

We don't tease each other in this class because in third grade we saw a puppet show about respecting each other's feelings. The main puppet was a dolphin. Basically the dolphin said that being the kind of person who hurt other people's feelings was way worse than having fat ears. I agree because it makes me hot all over when I see other kids tease Jimmy Collins for his ears, and because I like dolphins.

Mrs. Weiss calls on Jimmy a little reluctantly. She was on a roll and he stopped it.

"Yes, James?" she says. Nobody calls him James but her. James has the same amount of letters as Jimmy, but it feels bigger. And I think Jimmy Collins is just too little to be a James.

"You mean you want us to start thinking about what we want to be when we grow up?" Jimmy asks with a bored sigh. Everything seems to bore Jimmy. He sighs when he thinks other people are being stupid. Jimmy sighs a lot around me.

"I want you to start thinking of your place in the world," she says. She's talking through her teeth because her jaw is clenched.

Jimmy has a way of getting under your skin. He doesn't misbehave, not in the way Wilson Williams and Richie O'Brian do. They always make fart noises at general assemblies and get yelled at by the principal. I guess what Jimmy does is make everyone feel a little stupid. Even teachers.

"Instead of thinking of a job, I want you to think about how your talents could best serve the world," she continues. "Even if you have to invent a whole new career that they don't have a name for yet, I want you to do it. This year, I want you to find your destiny!"

I have to stop myself from jumping up and hollering

like Mrs. Weiss just scored a touchdown. I'm going to do this. I know I have a destiny, and I'm going to find it. Whatever it is.

"Now," Mrs. Weiss says, turning to the blackboard, "let's brainstorm."

Chapter Four

On Sundays the Bianchis go to church.

We all put on clean clothes, and then we rock-paper-scissors for who has to ride in the back of the van.

I always lose. Even when I win I lose, because Fay will hit me if she's stuck in the back of the van and I don't give her my spot in the station wagon. Not that the station wagon is any prize, let me tell you that much.

We have three cars in my family, and all of them are crappy (five Hail Marys). My dad has a pickup truck my uncle bought for him that we use on the farm, the van is the van, and the station wagon is left over from before we bought the van.

It's so old. It smells like spilled milk and melting plastic, but it did make it to the top of Mount Washington three summers ago when we took four days off after raspberry season for a summer vacation. We even splurged for a bumper sticker that says THIS CAR CLIMBED MOUNT WASHINGTON, but I don't think it counts if your car has to be pushed. What it should say is, *The Bianchis pushed a station wagon up Mount Washington because our crazy mother thought it would be fun to go camping.*

She was wrong, by the way. Camping is not fun like the camp Kristin described with the bunk beds and the clean sheets and the care packages. Real camping is not fun if you don't have hiking boots, or a sleeping bag, or a place to pee, and none of your damn (ten Hail Marys) sisters will move over and share their sleeping bag with you. Evangeline actually yelled at me because my teeth were chattering so loud it was keeping her up. Worst night of my life, I think. I tried to wake up Mom and Dad and tell them how cold I was, but they yelled at me and told me to go back to sleep.

All in all, we spent two days on the road and one and a half days out in the middle of the woods getting eaten by ticks. We haven't had a vacation since.

In the roshambo tournament for not sitting in the back of the van, I throw "rock" and get "papered" by Bridget, but I'm not too upset about it because at least I have new shoes. They aren't dress shoes. They're a kind of sneaker called Chuck Taylors, and I like them because they make me imagine my feet are in an old basketball movie.

My mom didn't want me to wear them to church with my dress, but seeing as how these are the only shoes I have, the Chuck Taylors won. I got them yesterday with Gina. She used the babysitting money she got on Friday night to buy them for me, because she said Mom would never get around to it because we don't have any money left for the month because Evangeline needed a new concert dress. It pisses Gina off when Mom spends all the money on Evangeline or Aurora, but it happens a lot because they have to look nicer than the rest of us because they have to go up onstage, and if they didn't have nice costumes and concert dresses, the family would be embarrassed.

When we run out of money, Gina gives Mom what she makes babysitting so Mom can buy groceries. Which is pretty much every week. Gina thinks Nora and I don't know she does it, but we do because we're snoops. We share a room with her and we know that no matter how long she's been babysitting other kids in the neighborhood, she only ever has five dollars for herself by the end of the weekend, tucked away under the broken ballerina in her music box. We know Gina doesn't spend all that money on herself going out, because she doesn't have any friends. Gina babysits a lot. Half the time I think she babysits for the money—I mean, of course it's for the money—but also I think she does it to get away from all of us.

Yesterday Gina said she couldn't stand looking at my shitty (fifteen Hail Marys, but for Gina) sneakers anymore, and she took me to the store and told me to pick out whatever I wanted under twenty dollars. There were other choices, but the Chuck Taylors were my favorite. They're white and they go with everything, even dresses, although no one else seems to agree with me. Bridget said they were ugly boy sneakers from five decades ago, but seeing as how most of my clothes are boy clothes from one decade ago, I think they make sense. I smile at my new white shoes all the way to church even though Fay tells me I look like a retard when I smile for no reason.

St. Agatha's is right in the center of our town. It's not a big church or anything, but it does have some stained-glass windows and a crucifix hanging above the altar that kind of freaks me out because Christ looks wicked skinny. All his ribs are showing and his face is hollowed out like he's about a thousand. Half the town comes to church every Sunday, but my town is really small, so it's not as crowded as you'd think.

Mass on Sunday is what my parents live for. My mom thumps away on the organ and my dad's an usher. The rest of us sit in the pews and try not to make too much noise.

That's harder than you'd think. Nothing Fay or

Bridget does is ever funny outside of church, but once we sit down in those pews and the incense gets burning and Mom is thundering away on that organ, everything becomes hilarious. Even just a look will start me giggling. And Bridget is the worst. She's got a rubber face. Somehow she can make herself look like other people. I don't know how she does it, but all she needs to do is point to someone sitting in the pews and the next second she looks just like that person.

You try not to laugh when all of a sudden Bridget looks like an eighty-year-old woman wearing a dumb hat. But my elder sisters don't care who started it. If they catch Nora and me laughing, they pinch us or twist our fingers. The worst part is that if the monkey bites and thumb crackers don't work, we laugh even harder, because once a giggle fit gets going, trying to stop it only makes it worse, and if even one peep comes out of us at the wrong time, our mom will hear it all the way up in the choral balcony.

Mom's got superhero hearing. She can hear our cat Geronimo walking across a carpet.

It's not that I want to be disrespectful, it's just that lately it all seems . . . well, kind of silly. The music and the smoke and the farty old priest blabbing on about the love of Christ and then he goes ahead and says we're all sinners and sinners go to hell, and then I got thinking that if I loved someone I'd never send them to hell, and a couple of months ago I realized I just don't see the point of coming to church in the first place. If I'm already going to hell—because if you're Catholic, you believe everyone was born a sinner—what does it matter what I do?

The more they try to explain Original Sin to me—and believe me, they've sat me down and tried to explain it a lot—the less I get it. Blaming a baby for something someone ate a million years ago is just about the dumbest thing I've ever heard, and I told them so.

That's when I got kicked out of Sunday school. I had to say I-don't-know-how-many rosaries, and my dad looked really sad. They let me back in after my mom went and had a talk with them, but even still my dad looks at me like he's worried I'm going to pop or something. I try to keep my mouth shut for his sake, but he's right. I can feel the questions building up in me, and one of these days a question they don't like is going to come flying out.

I make it through church with only one bruise on my thigh, from Gina. Monkey bite. Yeah, Gina pinches me too, sometimes, but I'm not afraid of her the way I am of Fay. With Gina you always know that she's doing it for your own good. She was just trying to get me to stop laughing when Bridget pointed out a woman picking a wedgie as she got up to get communion. Gina actually saved me from getting in worse trouble with Mom, and Gina always looks like she hates doing it, which is good. When Fay pinches you, you can tell she likes it. That's the scary part. She likes it, and you know if other people weren't around, she wouldn't stop.

Sometimes I think about what I might have to do someday if she doesn't stop hurting Nora or me. Well, at least I can leave church knowing one thing. Thinking the way I'm thinking means I'm definitely going to hell, so I don't have to worry about how many times I've taken the Lord's name in vain this week, because that horse has already left the barn.

Even when church is over it's not really over, at least not for my family. There's always some kind of coffee-and-doughnut thing in the basement or out on the lawn. The basement is for when it's raining. I hate going down there. It always smells like cigarettes from the alcoholics who go there to smoke on Saturday nights instead of getting drunk. Today is a nice day, so luckily, we're out on the lawn. The Bianchis attack the doughnuts. We don't get sweets at home. We only get sweets from the priests.

I get held up by my second-grade teacher, Mrs. Brown, so I don't get to the doughnut table in time. I really like Mrs. Brown. She says that she knows I'm going to accomplish Great Things. She talks in capital letters when she says it, too. I like that. I like that I know her well enough to know her punctuation. She was always big on punctuation.

When I get to the demolished doughnut table, I see Fay standing close by with three doughnuts in her hands. One of them is a Boston cream. Fay always gets the most doughnuts because she shoves everyone else out of the way and takes them. My empty stomach rumbles. Everything goes hazy for a second, and my ears start ringing. Oh boy. I'd better not faint.

"Fay?" I ask. "You gonna eat all those doughnuts by yourself?"

She licks her lips, still working on a cinnamon cruller. She takes another bite and chews. Her lips and tongue go everywhere. She's got a real long tongue, and she chews with her mouth open.

"Whaz one worth to ya?" she says. Her lips let loose a big, wet hunk of cruller. She doesn't even care that it lands on her dress.

I think about it because I'm hungry. Mom and Dad don't let us eat before Mass, because the Body of Christ should only be received on an empty stomach. I woke up at six and it's eleven now. That Boston cream looks darn good. But if I say yes, it's like the favor that never runs out.

The thing with Fay is, if you owe her for one little

thing, she thinks you owe her forever. Two weeks ago I asked her to help me take out the garbage because it was too heavy for me to lift, and after that she kept saying that I owe her for everything. She did it, like, a thousand times. She said, "Annie, give me the stamps Grandpa sent you because you owe me." And, "Annie, make my bed. You owe me."

The bed making I didn't mind so much. I spit on her pillow while I did it, so it's not like a favor at all. But the stamps are different. I like collecting stamps almost as much as I like collecting stickers. I have a book for each and I've just about filled both up. The stamps I do because my grandpa, my mom's dad, does them. When I get to see him, which isn't too often, we look through our collections together. He's got stamps from World War I, and I'm the only one of his grandkids who likes to collect stamps, so it's something we do together, which is nice.

I prefer to collect stickers, really. They've got unicorns and teddy bears on them and I think they're way prettier, but I don't mention that to Grandpa because he's a stamp man. And now I don't know what I'm going to tell him when he asks about the stamps Fay took. I guess I'll have to say I didn't get them.

I hate lying to Grandpa because I only see him every now and again on account of the fact that he lives miles and miles away, and because he's the only grandparent

I've ever known. My older sisters all knew Grandma, Grandpa's wife, and they tell me I got lucky she died before I was born. Miri says Grandma was even worse than Mom. You never knew when she was going to go off, and sometimes she would even go off on Mom. But I don't like to think about that.

Anyway, owing Fay favors didn't stop until yesterday when I told her no. I didn't want to give her the friendship bracelet that Kristin Gates gave to me. I just wouldn't do it. So she beat the stuffing out of me. Luckily, Nora got Aurora, and Aurora lost her mind when she saw that Fay was after me. Aurora looks delicate, but when she gets really angry she's scary. She's like Mom in that way.

One good thing about being the baby is that none of the bigger kids will let anyone hit me, not even a little bit. See, I'm like Switzerland. Everybody likes me, and they all know I'm too little to defend myself. Wish I could say the same for Nora, because Aurora just lets Fay whale on her.

Fay takes the last bite of her cruller. My vision blurs. They really ought to let us eat something before Mass. Fay licks her lizard lips. She's just waiting for me to crack.

"Annie?"

I turn around and see Jordan Dolan standing behind me with two doughnuts on a plate. One is a Boston cream. He jerks his head to the side, and in Jordan Dolan speak, that means *follow me*. So I follow him.

We sit down at a picnic table and Jordan takes a second paper plate off the bottom of his and carefully shifts the Boston cream onto it. I'm not surprised he brought two plates, or that he knows my favorite doughnut. I'm not even surprised he remembered to bring napkins.

The thing about Jordan is that everything he does is thought out way in advance. He's the exact opposite of me. I always wing it, but he says he likes that about me because I'm spontaneous and that's where some of the best ideas for our projects come from. Like when we built the volcano and I said we should put glitter in the goo and a tied-up Barbie doll at the top, like she was a human sacrifice. It looked awesome.

He gestures to Fay with his chin. "That's one of your sisters, isn't it?" he asks, breaking his doughnut in half. He likes plain old-fashioned ones. No glaze or anything.

"Yeah," I say, slinking down a little as Fay glares at us. I don't like the way she's looking at Jordan. It's like she's thinking of something mean.

Jordan looks back at Fay, and he doesn't look away. I've seen Jordan do this before with some of the boys from school, like Wilson Williams and Richie O'Brian, usually when they get after Jimmy because of his ears or Sarah Bernstein because she's Jewish. Jordan could make a pile of pillows uncomfortable just by staring at them long enough. Fay gives me a snotty look and then goes away. I realize I've been holding my breath and let it go.

"Thanks," I say, picking up my doughnut.

Jordan doesn't say anything, but that's okay because I don't need him to. I know he means *you're welcome*, even if we never say anything about this again. I enjoy my doughnut in peace and quiet for a while.

"Is it a sailboat?" I ask. I know he knows what I mean, because sometimes it takes days to have a conversation with Jordan Dolan, but we always pick right up where we left off and neither of us ever gets confused about it.

"Uh-huh," he says, rolling the spongy middle of his doughnut between his finger and thumb. "And it has an outboard motor. But I didn't build that. My dad did."

I nod. I don't know what an outboard is, but I get the gist of it.

"Nice Chucks," Jordan says.

I frown, and he points down at my shoes. Of course Jordan would know a cool name for them. Jordan knows all about cool stuff because he's rich. "Thanks. My sister bought them for me," I say, pulling my bright white feet out from under the table. "Not Fay, the mean one. Virginia, Gina. She bought them for me with her baby-sitting money yesterday. She's the bigger one."

He frowns and scans the crowd. I can practically see the wheels in his head turning. I like to watch Jordan think. He looks so serious it makes me want to crack a joke. Making Jordan laugh feels like laughing in church, except I don't get in trouble for it.

"The goth?" he asks, spotting her. I don't know what that is, but he's looking in Gina's direction, so I nod.

"Did you finish your homework yet?" I ask. He nods. Of course he finished. I haven't even started mine yet.

"Did you find your destiny yet?" he asks in return.

Oh yeah. I forgot about that. Now I feel bad because of Carl Sagan. He's counting on me.

"Not yet," I say with a shrug. "But it shouldn't be too hard. I mean, I've got sisters and a brother who are really good at a lot of stuff, so I should be really good at something, too."

"You're good at talking to people," Jordan says.

I scrunch up my face. "I like talking to people, but that isn't a *destiny*. That's, like, what you do at lunch," I say with a laugh.

Jordan just looks at me. Usually, I know what his looks mean, but this time I can't figure it out. It's weird not to know what Jordan's thinking, seeing as how I've been able to figure him out since the first week of first grade.

We were on the playground and Rob Winchell kept cutting the line for tetherball. Jordan just took hold of the ball and kept it, not letting anyone play until Rob agreed to go stand at the end. When the teachers tried to find out what was wrong, Jordan wouldn't say anything.

But see, Jordan was upset, and that's why he wasn't talking. Kind of like Nora, but different. She freezes up when you put too much pressure on her, but it's not that Jordan freezes up, he just refuses to talk when he can tell no one will understand him. He clams up.

So, anyway, I totally saw that the teachers needed to go away, so I told them that Jordan was handling it and we'd play in a second as soon as Rob Winchell stopped being such a ding-dong. And Jordan and I have been friends ever since, because I could tell that he hates anything that's unfair, like someone cutting the line, but he also likes to handle things himself without going and blabbing to the teachers.

"Annie, it's time to go," Nora says. She hovers over me, so I can tell I'm already late. I don't know how I managed to get late, because I feel like I just sat down with Jordan, but Nora hovering means I'm doing something wrong. Nora's a champion hoverer.

"Bye," I say, smiling at Jordan. "Thanks for the doughnut."

For a second it looks like Jordan wants to say something else, but then he just nods. I follow Nora to the car, worried. I feel like I didn't give him enough time to say what he needed to say, and now I'll never know.

"Was that your boyfriend?" Bridget teases as soon as she slides open the back door of the van. She and Fay are holding the door open, but they're blocking it, too.

"What did you give him for that doughnut?" Fay asks. Half of her upper lip is pulled up so I can see her fangy teeth.

Does she think I paid him? Jordan's not like that. He'd never charge me for a free doughnut. Fay definitely would, though.

"I didn't give him anything," I say, shrugging. "He's my lab partner."

Fay and Bridget look at each other and go, "OOOH," with their voices sliding all up and down.

"Just ignore them," Nora whispers in my ear.

"Fay and Bridget. Stop acting like idiots and get out of the way," Evangeline snaps. She's behind the wheel and JP is in the front seat.

They move so we can climb in, but not until Fay gives us the stink-eye. Great. Now she's going to get back at us for making Evie yell at her.

JP is looking out his window. "Is that him?" he asks, pointing at Jordan. He's walking across the parking lot with his hands in his pockets.

"Yeah," I say. We all watch him get into a shiny black BMW.

Evie and JP look at each other. Their eyebrows are practically on top of their heads.

"He's really cute," Evangeline says, like she's shocked.

I don't know what to say. Jordan is Jordan. I never thought about how he looked before. I mean, sure, I've thought about how he looks because I look at him all day, every day, seeing as how we're in every single class together. He's got brown hair that gets these big curls in it when he hasn't had a haircut in a while. He's got hazel eyes that are almost gold, and really long eyelashes like a girl. He used to get teased for them at the beginning of first grade, but that didn't last long. All of a sudden the bullies stopped teasing him and started avoiding him. I never found out why, though. I asked, and he clammed up. But that's Jordan for you.

"What do his parents do?" JP asks.

"Huh?" I ask. I forgot what we were talking about.

"Your lab partner. What do his parents do?"

"His mom's a lawyer. I have no idea what his dad does. Jordan told me he buys and sells companies. What do you call that?" I ask.

JP cranes his neck to look back at me. "Wealth," he says quietly.

"What's his house like?" Bridget asks, excited.

I shrug. "We always do our projects together in the ACT room at school," I tell them. "All the tools and supplies are there for us to use, and we don't even have to pay for them."

JP stares at me for a while. His lips are pressed together so I know he's upset about something. "Be careful," he tells me.

I laugh. "You don't have to tell *me*. Jordan already burned me once with the glue gun on accident last year when we were making a housing for the circuit board for his electricity project." I twist my left arm around so JP can see the pink scar just above my elbow. "See right there? It really hurt."

JP smiles suddenly, reaches back, and ruffles my hair. "I'll bet it did, Shrimpy."

"I think we've got a few more years," Evangeline says to JP. She sounds relieved.

I look between the two of them. "A few more years of what?" I ask, but no one answers. Evangeline just shakes her head when she turns the key in the ignition.

We have to wait behind Jordan's dad's BMW to get out of the parking lot. Everyone is really quiet while we drive home. I know what they're thinking, because I'm thinking it. They're thinking Jordan's dad's BMW probably has a radio that works and air-conditioning and, like, seats in the back and stuff.

When we get home, I feel kind of sad. I don't know why. Maybe it's because I haven't found my destiny. I bet Jordan knows his destiny already. He knows everything.

I have homework, but this is more important. I go downstairs and find Mom.

"Ma?" I ask. I have to say "Ma" about six more times for her to hear me, because she's busy both cooking dinner and unloading the dishwasher. I start to help her so she'll notice me.

"Ma," I try again when she looks at me, and I stop. It's been a long time since I've been this close to her—weeks, I think—and I forgot how nice she smells. Like powder and lemons.

"What, Annie?" she says tiredly.

"Why didn't I get ballet lessons?" I ask. "I could have been just as good at it as Aurora."

She looks down at the pot she's stirring. "You did get ballet lessons," she says.

I frown. "No, I didn't."

"Yes, you did. I took you to your first ballet class when you were five, like I did with all you kids, and you hated it. I didn't take you back because it would've been a waste of money. Besides, the teacher said all you did was daydream and hum to yourself while you looked in the mirror." She pushes past me to stack dishes over my head.

It was a long time ago, but I actually think I remember that. It was so boring until it was too hard. Seriously, I was tucking so much I thought any second I'd see the back of my own bum peeking up at me from between my legs. My thighs ached for days afterward.

"If you're going to help, help," Mom scolds, motioning for me to move. "Clear off the table."

I start gathering up piles of . . . I have no idea what all this is. Mail, sheet music, rosary beads, a dried-out set of toy watercolors, and other "odds and ends" (as Mom calls them) that seem to collect wherever my mother is. I start carrying piles of stuff into the sewing room/ study, but there's no place to put any of it. The desk is buried and so's the chair, and there's all kinds of knitting and needlepoint baskets cluttering up the sewing table, so I just start to stack Mom's junk on the floor.

"What about piano? I could have been like Evie," I say when I come back in the kitchen. She smiles and rolls her eyes. "What?" I ask.

"You're tone-deaf, Annie. You couldn't carry a tune in a bucket."

I didn't know I was tone-deaf. Maybe that's why everyone gives me that look when I sing along to U2 or the Police and especially that song "We Belong" by Pat Benatar. (It took me forever to figure out she was saying, "We belong to the light, we belong to the THUNDER."

I used to just say *DUM-DA* really loud when that part came.) Well, at least now I know why.

"Then what about—"

She cuts me off. "Soccer, like your brother? You don't know your left from your right. I took you to soccer when you were five. The coach told you to run one way, and you ran the other like your hair was on fire." She turns away from me like I'm hassling her. "You're a menace at sports. You can't even go down a Slip 'N Slide without injuring yourself so badly the whole town asked if we'd been in a car accident."

Okay, now that's unfair. The Slip 'N Slide thing was not my fault. Two summers ago Dad told us the Slip 'N Slide was ruining the lawn, so we weren't to use it anymore, but Fay didn't want to stop, so she figured if we moved it to the driveway, we wouldn't hurt the grass. Our driveway is a long, steep hill, and Fay promised it'd be like going down a slide at a water park. At the last second she told me to go down first to test it out, and so I charged at full speed and only realized my mistake when I was out of wet plastic, with no way to stop myself, and about to skid across concrete. I was in a bikini.

"The only thing you might be good at is distance running," my mom continues, "but only because once you actually start something, which is rare, you're too stubborn to stop."

I didn't know I was stubborn. Why doesn't anybody tell me these things? "Well, what about—"

She turns to face me. And she's actually looking in my eyes, so I shut up. If it's been weeks since I've been near her, it's probably been months since she's looked me right in the eye. I think the last time I had all of her attention (okay, most of it) was when I had the stomach flu so bad they almost had to take me to the hospital. *Star Wars* was on TV for the first time, and she hadn't yet banned us from watching it. Mom let me put my head in her lap while she folded laundry. It was awesome. Well, except for the cramps and the fever and the barfing, but other than that, it was awesome.

Was that second grade? Had to be. Jordan gave me a get-well card he made out of construction paper, and he spelled *well* with only one *L*. It was probably the last time Jordan Dolan misspelled anything.

My mom's still waiting for me to talk, but I'm still thinking how nice it was to put my head in her lap. When you're the youngest of nine kids, you never see your parents. And they hardly ever really see you, either, even if they're looking right at you.

"What? What do you want to do, Annie? What are you good at?"

I got nothing. If Fay were in the room, she'd call me

a mouth breather because of how my jaw is hanging open. I shut it with a snap.

"I don't know. But I'm going to find out," I say.

"If you can pay for it yourself, I'm all for it," she says. She turns toward the stove. "Now will you get out from underfoot? I have work to do."

She's not trying to be mean. I know it seems like she is, but Mom is always spread thin. It's like nothing she does is what she wants to do, and everything you add to that, even if it's just talking, could be the last straw for her. It's not her fault. She didn't choose me any more than I chose her.

Miri told me. She said Mom held it together before she had Bridget, and then after, she couldn't stop crying. Then she just gave up on all of us and lost it. If she could have stopped after JP, I think everything would have been okay. Everyone says Mom and Dad should have stopped after having a boy. I know that means I wouldn't have been born, but that doesn't bother me. It's not like I'd know the difference.

Chapter Five

At some point in September, the whole family visits the two tias.

They're not my aunts, or even my father's aunts, but they are related to me. I think, anyway. See, it's tough to tell. Tia Nina and Tia Olga are from the "Old Country," and they're like great-aunts or something. I don't think either of them was my nonna's sister, but it's hard to tell sometimes because all the old Italians grew up in the same village in northern Italy. Everyone in that village was from one of two families that intermarried as long as the cousins weren't *too* close.

It's gross, I know. But I guess this village was out in the middle of nowhere and there weren't any other options, unless you went over a ton of mountains and married an Austrian, and Italians don't like how Austrians talk, or at least my relatives didn't.

Okay. So. Everyone had to leave this village after it was pretty much flattened during World War I, and they all promised to look out for each other's children in case someone died on the boat ride to America, and that's why it doesn't matter if they're really my aunts or not because they swore a blood oath and Italians are just bananas when it comes to oaths. Which is weird considering they always seem to be making them. Makes you wonder how they keep track of them all.

I can't tell you how many times I've sat in Tia Nina's kitchen and seen her raise her right hand like she's pledging allegiance and haul herself up next to her ancient wood-burning cast-iron stove and babble something in Italian that my eldest sisters (who learned Italian, but the younger ones didn't, because Dad got too busy working all the time and was never around to teach us) tell me is her swearing her right hand to God that so-and-so from the old country gave the evil eye to her favorite goat and killed it fifty years ago. And then she'll open the stove door and spit into the fire.

They're just . . . nuts. And my father would do anything for them, so that means the rest of us would, too.

Tia Nina and Tia Olga wear all black dresses because they're both widows. They have no teeth, and would probably be about six feet tall if you stacked one on top of the other. They don't speak English, but they don't have to with us kids, because all we're allowed to do in Tia Nina's kitchen is sit quietly and eat *pizzelle*, which are anise-flavored cookies that are flat and shaped like snowflakes. I like them because they taste like licorice.

The only question that I ever have to answer the two tias is this: *Are you being a good girl?* My father translates, and I nod my head and say *sì*.

That's it. And I get a truckload of *pizzelle*, because the two tias try to stuff me blind with them anyways because they think I'm skinny. Which they swear (their right hands to God) will keep me from getting a husband. They're both shaped like meatballs, and that's why their husbands loved them so much. Or that's what Miriam told me they said right before they both started cackling like a couple of wicked witches.

I like the two tias. They scare the crap (five Hail Marys) out of me, but they both have really kind eyes somewhere under all those wrinkles. And Tia Nina has green eyes just like Dad and me.

Miriam always comes back from MIT for the visit to the tias, but I don't know why she does unless it's to translate for us kids. Miri always seems a little put out around them. She gets snappy, although maybe I'm the only one to really notice, because she works so hard to hide it.

We have something like arranged seating when we all cram ourselves into one of the tias' kitchens. This year we're at Tia Nina's, and Tia Nina is the one with the big black stove that she never seems to be more than a few steps from. I always sit next to Miriam. I used to sit on her lap when I was littler, because she's the eldest and I'm the youngest. She's my sister, but more like my mom than Mom ever was. My earliest memory is sitting on Miri's lap in Tia Nina's kitchen. I was wearing a white lace dress.

Miri says there's no way I can remember that because it was my first birthday, which is always a big party because Italians from the Old Country don't really admit you're alive until after you've survived through your first year, I guess because most of their babies didn't. But I do remember it. I remember calling Miri "Mama," and I remember the tias frowning at Mom for it. That's why the tias still scare me a little. I remember their frowns.

They still frown at my mom a lot. See, Mom's Irish. And for some reason, if she'd been an Italian girl, she wouldn't have had so many kids and been such a burden on my dad. No one's ever said it, not out loud anyways, but I can feel it. I can *see* it, for crying out loud. Mom never gets closer than two feet to any of her in-laws—not the tias, not Dad's brother, Uncle Antonio, or his wife, Aunt Constance. They don't talk, they don't touch, and they barely like sitting in the same room. Even now Mom's sitting as far away from the big black stove as you can get. Aurora is sitting next to her, as usual.

Aurora always sits next to Mom and translates for her. Mom always holds Aurora's hand whenever they sit next to each other. Mom loves Aurora the most, and who can blame her? Aurora is beautiful.

I don't know why, but the *pizzelle* aren't doing it for me this year. I'm nibbling around the edges to be polite, but really, I'm looking at Miri. I've missed her a lot since she left. She comes back a ton to see us all, but it's not the same. I used to sleep in her bed with her when it got really cold, and now it's just the top bunk and me, although I have stopped falling out of it all the time. Now falling's just a special-occasion thing.

Miri isn't even trying to hide how frustrated she is. She keeps looking at Mom and Aurora and then back at the tias. She's grinding her teeth. She used to do that in her sleep when she was having a nightmare.

"What?" I whisper to her, hiding my totally illegal speaking behind my uneaten *pizzelle*. Miri grinds her teeth some more. I reach down and squeeze her fingers.

She's bitten right through the side of her thumb till it bled. I do that sometimes. I bite or pick my fingers when I'm anxious.

She shifts in her seat to hide our conversation. "I'm sick of this," she whispers. Her dark brown eyes are too bright. I think she might cry. "Not one of them helped."

I take a giant bite of my *pizzelle* and choke on it, but I swallow like crazy, trying to stuff it down. My eyes water and my voice is all wheezy when I ask, "Helped what?"

"Helped Mom," Miri says, raising her voice. My dad heard her speak. Kids aren't allowed to speak unless spoken to around the tias.

I figure I've got a mouth full of *pizzelle* and nothing to lose. The tias think I'm strange anyhow on account of the fact that they always catch me smiling and humming to myself because I'm bored.

I let the cough go and start hacking away, spewing *pizzelle* all over the place. Miri starts banging on my back and everybody jumps up. Somebody hands me water, which, when you think about it, makes no sense. If you're choking on something, how would wetting it help?

Boogers are streaming out of my nose, and so many people are thumping on me you'd think I was a dusty rug. Miri finally drags me outside. She's talking in Italian and shooing everyone else away. They go when she tells them to go because they all know that she's in charge of me, like always. After a while I've settled down.

"You okay?" Miri asks. She's wiping my drippy face with her sleeve. I nod and she smiles at me. "Thanks for covering for me."

"No problem," I wheeze, blinking back a few more choke-tears.

We sit down on the ground and look at the darkening farmland. This isn't our farm; it's our relatives', the Iruzzis'. It's one town over from ours. They have way more land than we do, but it isn't prettier. I wait, because I can tell Miri has something to say, but she's always been slow to talk. Now that I think of it, Miri is like Dad. And Jordan.

She looks up at the sunset sky. "I'm so sorry, Annie," she says.

As far as I can tell, Miri has never done anything to be sorry about. "For what?" I ask.

"I can't do it anymore."

"Do what?"

She looks at me and smiles like she's going to cry. "Did you know I was your age when you were born?"

It gets dark in a second. We even see the green flash from the ocean side of the Iruzzi farm, that last blip of the sun disappearing. It's so pretty it makes us watch for just a moment, which is good because I can hardly understand what it would have been like for me to have a baby, like Miri had me. I mean, I know I'm not hers. But I *was* hers. I guess it is pretty strange. None of my friends got raised by their big sisters. I just never really thought about it before because that's the way it always was. But it wasn't normal. And it wasn't really fair to Miri.

"No one helped," she says. The dark keeps falling on her as she talks, but I can see her because I know every expression on her face so well I could see her without eyes, probably. "No one helped Mom. No one helped me. I was ten and I had a newborn. I fed you. I bathed you. We slept in the same bed and I was there when you cried. If I hadn't been there . . ."

She looks at me for a long time. I can feel the dew seeping into my clothes. I can smell the apples in the orchard. The grass is spiky under my hot hands.

"I can't do it anymore," Miri says. I can't see her tears, but I can feel them. "I'm so sorry. I never should have been your mother. A ten-year-old girl should not be left with a newborn baby."

She lowers her head like she's ashamed of herself. Like she did something wrong.

"Why not? You did great."

I say *great*, but it sounds kind of silly and small compared to what she did for me. I want to say more. I want to tell her everything I feel about her, but I don't know what to say and I'm scared that it won't be enough. I have a terrible feeling right now.

She shakes her head. "I burned you." I can barely hear her. It's like her voice has turned inside out. "Mom told me to do the dishes and wash the baby, so I filled the sink up with water for the dishes, but I was so tired. You'd been up all night and I was so tired."

Miri drops her head and cries in that way we do. No sound. But it's coming up from her feet and running all through her like lightning. The harder she cries, the quieter she gets. Miri's the master at hiding it, even better than Nora.

She keeps going. "You were screaming and reaching for me and I kept pushing you into the water again and again. I was so mad at you for fighting me. And then my hand touched the water and I felt how hot it was."

She cries for a long time, her body curling and rolling over her sobs, and she still isn't making a sound. When Miri cries, it hurts me worse than crying myself.

"I don't remember any of that. All I remember is that you were awesome to me," I tell her. I'm scared and I need to make her smile. I have to be able to make her happy, because I owe her for everything. My whole life, actually, and I can already tell something bad is about to happen and I don't want it to. I just want to make her laugh so hard she forgets this whole thing. I nudge her with my shoulder and smile at her out of the corner of my mouth. "You only dropped me on my head, like, six times."

I'm trying to joke, but it doesn't sound funny. I don't feel very funny right now. She hugs me anyway. And then she sniffs and rubs her eyes, first left, then right, then left again like the tears won't stop just yet, but they might soon. The moon is rising.

"I don't blame Mom. It's all she knew," she says after a long time. "You weren't around when Mom's mom was still alive, but she was even worse." She looks at me and her eyes are big and scared. "I don't want to be like them."

"You could never be," I tell her. "Look, if anyone would know, it would be me, right? You were an awesome mom."

"Oh, Annie." She sighs and smiles. "I'm going to miss you." She puts her arm around me. "You were a good baby, but I was never your mother and I never got to be a kid." She pulls away so she can see me in the moonlight.

I don't know what to do, so I put my head on her shoulder and pretend we're going to stay like this. I know she's going to go away for a long time, and I know that's why she's telling me all this.

"Write to me," I whisper.

A wet, sobby laugh breaks out of her. "I will. And if you ever really need me, I'll be at MIT, okay? You can always come to me, Annie."

I look down and swallow. "But you won't be coming home anymore."

"No. I'm getting out while I still can."

After a long while Miri gets into the old blue Chevy Nova that used to belong to my aunt Mary Perpetua (my mom's sister, and totally Irish) and drives south toward Boston. I sit in the grass for a long time—hours, it feels like—because I don't really want to go back in there with all those people who say they're family but never did anything to help Miri. Or my mom. I never needed someone to swear a blood oath for me. I just needed someone to give me a bath.

A light goes on from the house. "She's out here," JP says behind me. I hear him walking toward me. "Where's Miriam?" he asks, standing over me.

"Oh. She had a test or something, so she had to get back to school," I say.

JP looks down on me for just long enough to tell me he knows I'm lying.

"You can talk to me, you know," he says, and I know I can because JP has never laughed at me when I've told him something, even if it was just silly kid stuff.

"Miri just told me she's going away for a while." I look up and see JP nod. Miri must have already told him.

"Are you upset about that?" he asks.

I shrug. "I'm not surprised" is all I'll say. I don't want to get into it with JP and start crying or something. Everyone's about to come out here.

He reaches a hand down. "Come on, Shrimpy. It's time to go home."

He pulls me up and puts an arm over my shoulder, bumping me with his hip and messing with me until I laugh and chase him to the car. JP always makes me feel better. He hardly ever says he loves me, but he always makes me feel like he's saying it, you know?

The whole car ride home I think about my destiny. It better be a great one, for Miri's sake.

When we get home, Nora practically runs upstairs to her room. Fay follows her, and I can tell from the look on her face that something isn't right. I start to go up the stairs after them, but Bridget gets in my way.

"Want to play cards?" she asks me.

"No," I say. "I want to go to bed."

"It's early," she says, grabbing my hand and dragging me into the playroom. "Play one game with me and then go to bed."

I'm getting anxious now. I don't know how I know

something bad is going on except that Bridget never pays attention to me in a nice way. I pull my arm out of Bridget's hand and run upstairs.

When I get to our room, it's too late. Nora's face is all red and she's cradling her left arm with her right like it's a dead animal and Fay is walking out of our room with something in her hand. Fay looks at me to see what I'm going to do. She's close enough now that I can see what she's got. It's a birthday card. Fay's birthday isn't until summer, but Nora's birthday is next week.

Fay's still staring at me, and I realize I'm blocking the door. She gets really close to me and speaks quietly.

"Nora gave this to me, right?" she says.

I swallow and look down. She grabs one of my wrists and twists. It hurts, a lot. That's bad enough, but the worst thing is that it doesn't leave any kind of mark. No red spots like a pinch or a burn, and no bruises like a punch or a kick. A twisted arm just hurts and hurts until the person stops, and when it's over, there's no proof it ever happened.

"She *gave* me her birthday money from the two tias. Right?" Fay repeats. She doesn't even sound angry, because she's not. Because she knows she's going to win.

I see Nora holding her hurt arm across her body. I have to nod. When I do, Fay lets me go and walks away, probably to go downstairs like nothing happened.

Nora won't look at me. This is just like when Fay took her First Communion money. Nora will act like she hates me for a while because she needs someone to hate, and she couldn't possibly hate Fay any more than she already does.

Chapter Six

There's going to be a teacher in space.

Christa McAuliffe is going to ride on the space shuttle *Challenger*, and she's going to be the first teacher in space. She was selected and I saw it on the news last night, and I can't stop thinking about it because if someone who isn't an astronaut can go into space, anyone can go. That is so freaking awesome.

When Kristin Gates gets on the bus, I can see the excited look on her face. I wave to her, and she comes rushing to me with her Trapper Keeper clutched to her chest.

"Did you hear?" she says. She's so excited she can hardly catch a breath.

"Yes!" I reply. "I could barely sleep last night."

"Me either!" Kristin squeals. "I wonder who's going to ask me."

Hang on. I don't think we're talking about the same thing, but I can't say anything about it now or I'll look stupid.

She gives me a sneaky smile and elbows me. "I wish Jordan would, but we all know he's going to ask you."

I smile and nod and shake my head and shrug all at the same time, hoping Kristin will pick whichever gesture is the right one until I can figure out what she's talking about.

"How did you hear?" I ask, fishing for a clue.

"My mom's on the school board," Kristin says, like I should know that. "She said that sixth and seventh are going to be combined this year on Saturday night, so that leaves Friday night for us."

Uh . . . still no idea what's going on.

"So, how did you find out?" she asks. Her tiny nose is scrunched up. It's cute on her. If I did it, I'd look like an anteater. I have a beak where Kristin has a button.

She's still waiting for an answer. I remember her saying something about somebody asking her something. "So who do you think will ask you?" I say to distract her.

Kristin sighs and then launches into a list of all the boys in our grade. I keep saying "Uh-huh" and "Na-uh!" when it feels like that's what she's looking for. Luckily, she keeps chattering the whole way to school and off the bus and halfway down the hallway.

"It's going to be this Friday after school," Karen Green says as she runs toward us. "I hope Chris Lawrence asks me."

"Then why don't you ask him?" Samantha Schnabel replies, rolling her eyes. She looks down the hall and giggles suddenly. "Jordan Dolan is walking toward us," she says, dropping her chin and blushing.

What the hell (five Hail Marys) has happened to all my friends?

I turn around to include Jordan and see he's just as confused as I am. He looks around at all the girls staring at him. I can tell he's getting uncomfortable, so I say the first thing that pops into my head.

"Did you see the news last night?" I ask him.

"Christa McAuliffe," he blurts out, looking relieved. "Isn't it awesome?"

"I know, right?" I say, nodding at him and so happy that I'm finally part of a conversation I can understand. "First teacher in space."

"I wonder if she'll be doing experiments up there," Jordan says. His eyes are all starry.

"Yeah, like, seeing if the same experiments we do in science class have the same results in space."

"What if they're different?" he asks.

Jordan and I grin at each other, thinking about how cool that would be. We'd have to reinvent science, because if science doesn't work everywhere, it doesn't work at all. It gets quiet again. I notice that Kristin, Samantha, and Karen are staring at us.

"Don't you want to ask Annie something?" Kristin says to Jordan.

Jordan clams up. When Jordan clams up, it's not just that he stops talking. He shuts his face off, too, so you can't even get a hint of what he's thinking.

The bell rings and we all have to rush to homeroom. Right before we take our seats, Kristin grabs my arm.

"I'm so sorry, Annie. I didn't mean to embarrass you," she whispers. "I really thought he'd ask you."

"It's okay," I say, still lost. I smile at her really big while I take my seat behind Jordan so she doesn't feel bad anymore.

I still don't know four periods later when I walk into the lunchroom, but I find out.

The whole cafeteria has been plastered with posters that say FIFTH GRADE HALLOWEEN DANCE FRIDAY NIGHT!!! And others that say SIXTH AND SEVENTH COMBINED HALLOWEEN DANCE SATURDAY NIGHT!!!

Oh.

The word *dance* is everywhere. It keeps repeating in my head until it's just a sound that rhymes with *pants* and *ants*. Ants-in-the-pants dance. Ha!

I'm smiling when I sit down at the lunch table with everyone.

"Oh my God, he asked you," Karen says with way too many high notes and not enough low notes in her voice.

"Huh?" I say, still singing the ants-in-the-pants dance in my head.

"Jordan asked you to the dance," Samantha translates. She's got her arms crossed and her lips are as tight as the knot on a balloon.

"No he didn't," I say, sitting.

Kristin reaches out and squeezes my hand. "Sorry," she says.

"Why?" I ask.

I pull out my sandwich. I can immediately tell something's wrong with it. I peel apart the edges of the bread and see my mom's mistake. There's no meat or cheese or even a tomato in here. My mom made me a mayonnaise sandwich. My mom's a really forgetful person. She's forgotten to make my lunch before, but remembering the mayo and forgetting the meat? This is a new one. My mother is always coming up with new and interesting ways to forget about me.

I move my tongue around my mouth, trying to gauge my hunger vs. the gross-out factor of eating a mayonnaise sandwich. I shove the pieces back together before my friends can think maybe I'm too poor to put anything in my sandwiches.

"Do you want to talk about it?" Sarah asks.

Damn (ten Hail Marys). They must have seen my meatless sandwich. "I should have packed my own lunch. It's no big deal," I say. They look confused.

"About *Jordan*," Samantha says. As soon as his name is out, she looks up and slaps a hand over her mouth. Everybody gasps and looks behind me.

"Annie?"

I turn around to see Jordan. "Hi," I say.

"You wanna go to the dance?" he asks.

I shrug. I like dancing, I've just never done it in front of other people before. "I hadn't really thought about it," I say.

"Think about it."

"Okay. I will."

"Good," he says, and walks back to a table full of boys, who are all staring at him. A second after he sits down, the boys turn to stare at me.

Boys are strange.

Now, how am I going to fix this sandwich?

"That was the coolest thing I've ever seen," says Sarah Bernstein. "You were like, *whatever.* And he was like, *whatever.*" She sucks air through her teeth like she burned herself.

I look around the table. My friends are all staring at me. I think I've missed something here. All I know is Samantha's pissed off again, and Kristin is trying not to look sad.

"He made you wait four whole periods," Karen says. "You played it perfectly, Annie."

Eat your sandwich, dummy, and try to put the facts in order. One: nobody cares about Christa McAuliffe but Jordan and me. Two: there is a Halloween Dance. Three: Jordan asked me if I was going to it. Four: Oh.

The mayonnaise sandwich turns to glue in my mouth. Why am I so slow?

"Annie? Are you okay?" Kristin asks.

I swallow. "Do you think Jordan was asking me to the dance?"

"Oh my God," Samantha says. She sighs and slumps in her chair, shaking her head at me.

Kristin shoots Samantha an angry look. "Yes," she says, answering my question. "And you told him you'd think about it."

That was a lucky break. I nod for a while. "So, how does this work? Going to a dance with someone, I mean."

The girls lean in, excited. "Well, first you have to buy a dress," Karen says.

Buy. A dress. With money?

"Then he'll have his mom drive him to your house and they'll pick you up," Sarah says. "His mom might come inside to meet your mom."

My mom. His mom. Jordan. In my *house*. A panic light starts flashing in my head. Sirens clang. Some old movie actor shoots at a giant squid and screams, "Abandon ship!"

I crumple up the rest of the mayonnaise sandwich in its brown paper bag and march over to Jordan's table. He turns and smiles at me, but his smile disappears when he sees my face.

"No," I say.

I run out of the cafeteria.

Jordan won't look at me for the rest of the day. He doesn't even glance in my direction once, and I know he doesn't because I spend the last three periods trying to catch his eye and make him smile or something.

I feel awful. He looks so angry. The only time Jordan's ever been angry with me was when I said I wanted Walter Mondale to win because then Geraldine Ferraro would be the first woman vice president, and Jordan said that picking a president because of the vice president didn't make any sense, and I told Jordan that *he* didn't make any sense.

We were mad at each other for two whole days, and then I asked him to help me build a giant pendulum in the gym so we could demonstrate the rotation of the Earth and we both forgot about the Geraldine Ferraro thing.

I have the feeling that this time neither of us is going to just forget about it. Something's changed. I don't like it.

"What's the matter with you?" Nora asks as we stand in line for the bus. She's still hating me instead of Fay, or because I was there, or just because she kinda hates everyone right now, so there's no point in trying to tell her what happened, because she'll just be mean about it.

"Nothing," I lie, trying to look two lines over to find Jordan, but I don't see him anywhere. Nora keeps looking at me and frowning as we get on the bus.

"You're coming over to my place after school," Kristin says. I don't really feel like company, but Kristin won't let it go. "We'll eat Fruit Roll-Ups and watch *General Hospital*," she says, taking my hand and dragging me off the bus at her stop.

Kristin is a latchkey kid. Both her parents work, so she has the whole house to herself when she gets home from school. Usually I love coming over to her place. It's like going to a different planet—a clean, quiet planet with lots of food.

All the furniture matches. The chairs have red cushions on them. The red cushions go with the red drapes. The red drapes go with the flowery wallpaper that Kristin once told me was from Laura Ashley. I don't know who Laura Ashley is, but I know you're supposed to say her name in a whisper. All the dishes match, and none of them are chipped. The pots are so pretty they hang them from the ceiling so everyone can see. Even the plants are just the right shade of green. All the plants in my house died long ago, probably because our cat, Geronimo, wouldn't stop peeing in them.

Kristin always has the apple cinnamon Fruit Roll-Ups that I really like and never get at home, but even though I didn't eat lunch, I'm not at all hungry. It's like my stomach has a rock in it.

"You think I don't know why you turned Jordan down, but I do," Kristin says.

I laugh. "Well, if you understand, you'd better explain it to me, because I haven't understood one thing all damn"—(ten Hail Marys)—"day."

Kristin looks at me from across the table. "How long have we been friends?" she asks me.

I shrug. "Since first grade," I answer.

"How many times have I been in your house?"

"Never," I say. She just looks at me. "You'd hate it."

"You always say that, Annie."

One little part of me wants to tell her. She's a good friend and she's just trying to help. The rest of me sees this kitchen and wants to stay here and pretend I belong here. If she knows the truth, I won't even get to pretend I'm just like her and that everything is safe and smells nice and there isn't shit (fifteen Hail Marys) all over the place. I cross my arms over the rock in my stomach.

"I just don't want to go to the dance. That's why I said no."

Kristin's shoulders slump. "Fine," she says. "Let's watch *General Hospital*."

I have no idea why the people in this show always look like they're about to cry. I don't understand what's going on, but that seems to be my whole day right there. All I can tell is that all the crying is usually over a boy.

It dawns on me that this is why all my friends know about school dances and what you're supposed to do if a boy asks you out. All my friends come home and watch soap operas all afternoon. Look, if I had nothing else to do when I got home but think about boys and all I did was watch soap operas to practice, I'd probably never have made such a fool of myself in school today about Jordan.

But we don't watch soap operas in my house. And when I go home, I've got other things to think about.

The show ends, and Kristin uses the remote to turn off the TV. In my house, I'm the remote. How can someone like Kristin ever understand that?

"You should probably call Jordan tonight and apologize for turning him down in front of all his friends like that," Kristin says. "You really embarrassed him."

I nod, but I don't call Jordan when I get home, because what would I say? I can't tell him the truth about why I did it. Plus, I've never called Jordan on the telephone before.

When I get to school the next day, it's like Jordan doesn't even know me. After homeroom, when he doesn't turn around to say hi, I know I can't sit behind him anymore. First period I change seats. I'll sit at the front of the class with Jimmy Collins from now on so I can't stare at Jordan even if I want to. I still feel like there's a rock in my stomach, but it's a little better than it was yesterday, and maybe in a couple of weeks it'll be gone. And then it'll be like Jordan and I were never friends to begin with.

At lunch I find out Jordan Dolan is going to the Halloween Dance with Kristin Gates. I smile and say, "That's great."

Friday and the Halloween Dance come and go, and

it's a good thing I didn't go, because Saturday I have to go to the farm really early with my family and pick tomatoes.

Remember how I said it was hot on the farm? Well, it is, unless it's cold. Today it's really cold and wet. Tonight's actually Halloween and I love Halloween, usually, but this year I don't really care.

I pick a ton of tomatoes, probably because I don't daydream at all. I work so hard my dad notices. He smiles at me, which is nice. I don't go home after lunch. Instead I offer to stay late with him to help ready the back field for winter. We plow under the yellowing cornstalks that have already been picked clean.

The ground is heavy with water, and the plow shears keep kicking up. Every time they do, I have to jump off the tractor, knock the earth off a blade that's practically bigger than me, and pull it back down until it locks into place. We're at it for hours.

I ride home alone with my dad. We don't talk or anything, but it's nice to sit next to him in the truck. I never really get to just sit with him like right now. It almost makes me feel better about Jordan, except it doesn't because I don't think anything ever really will. I'm so tired when I get home I can barely eat or wash up or care that other kids are out trick-or-treating.

I'm too old for that anymore, anyway.

Chapter Seven

Christmastime in my family is sort of a mixed bag.

This year everyone wants me to play Mary in the Nativity play. I don't know if I want to do it or not, because I like sitting next to my mother when she plays the organ. But when the new priest, Father Joe (he's super young and in charge of the youth outreach program my brother is a part of, and my brother is always talking about him) asks me to read the lines with him, I can see how excited he is about me being Mary, so I agree.

Just like that, I'm Mary. I have to go to rehearsal and stuff, but it's right before choir practice, so I can still turn pages for my mom.

Everyone keeps saying how good I am. I don't know how anyone can tell, with me only having three lines, but after a couple of rehearsals, I realize I like being told I'm good at something. And Father Joe keeps saying how important what I'm doing is. Father Joe has this really hyper way of talking that's still cool, because he's way younger than Mrs. Weiss and he uses words like *awesome* without sounding like he's trying too hard. He keeps talking like this is my destiny.

And then I think—maybe it is! After all, Carl Sagan was kind of an actor. Well, not really an actor, but he did have a TV show, so maybe I should, too. I haven't figured out all the details yet, but I've got time. There are still months and months of school left.

I'm so caught up in all the churchy stuff I have to do that I totally forget about the exams we have to take right before we go home for the long winter break. I realize my mistake as soon as I stroll into Mrs. Weiss's class. Everyone is rereading their textbooks, and it hits me. I didn't remember. Usually I don't need to remember to study because I don't need to study, but I can already tell that the tests this year are going to be different than they used to be. These tests are going to be bigger than any test I've ever taken before.

I get cold all over and then I get really hot. I wander to my seat up front with Jimmy Collins, wishing like crazy that today isn't what I think it is. Jimmy looks at me.

"What's wrong with you?" he asks.

"Are exams today?" I ask.

Jimmy sighs, and I realize I said that a little louder than I should have. I look around. Pretty much the whole classroom is looking back at me.

Okay, there are only eight of us in Mrs. Weiss's class, but still, *Jordan* looks at me, and he hasn't looked at me in months.

Now I'm more sad than I am scared. And I'm not sad because I know that if Jordan and I were still friends, he'd have reminded me to study yesterday, because he knows I always forget stuff like this. I'm sad just because we aren't friends. He looks away with his face all clammed up, and I sit down at my desk and I'm not even worried anymore, because I'm too busy being upset about Jordan to be upset about not studying.

Mrs. Weiss comes in just as the bell is ringing and tells us, "Put your books away. No more talking." And she starts placing the mimeographed tests facedown on each of our desks.

"Got a pencil?" I whisper to Jimmy. He sighs again and shakes his head.

I look around the room for someone else to ask. Kristin shrugs at me. I can see she only has one on her desk in front of her. Jordan has about five, all presharpened and lined up evenly in front of him, and his eraser is holding them up on the slanted desk. I always think of

Jordan when I smell eraser crumbs. Probably because when we do our projects together, he usually takes down all the ideas that I come up with because he knows how I'm dyslexic and can't write all that fast.

Jordan sees me looking at his pencils, and I know all I have to do is ask him and he'll give me one. But then I think maybe he won't. And if he doesn't, I'll probably start crying, because I'm almost crying right now as it is. I look away from him and raise my hand.

"Mrs. Weiss? May I borrow a pencil?" I ask her.

Mrs. Weiss gives me the cross look she saves for troublemakers who make fart noises during school assembly.

"I told everyone to bring pencils today, Antoinette. That includes you," she tells me.

Jordan is looking out the windows, and his leg is bouncing up and down. He only does that when he's really annoyed.

"I know. I forgot," I say. My face just keeps getting hotter and hotter. It's like a dream I had once where I showed up to school naked. Actually, I think this is worse. "May I borrow one? So I can take the test?"

She crosses her arms and shakes her head. "You have to start being more responsible, Antoinette. You have an incredible imagination, but you need to start thinking about the present moment more than your daydreams. I'm afraid I can't lend you a pencil."

"Okay," I say. My voice sounds all broken and strange. I wonder if she's going to flunk me and kick me out of ACT. I probably never should have been in this class anyways.

But it still isn't fair, and I'm just realizing that this second.

Looking around, I notice how everyone else in this class has backpacks and pencil cases and lunch boxes. All their stuff is neat and tidy, and I know for a fact that Kristin's mom packs her backpack for her in the morning and reminds her to do her homework the night before, and my mom has never once done that for me. And I've never even owned a backpack or a pencil case or a Trapper Keeper. My mom didn't even buy me new *shoes* this year before school, why the hell (five Hail Marys) would she buy me a pencil case and make sure I've got it with me when I walk out the door?

Half the time, I have no idea where my parents are when I leave for school in the morning. I can go weeks without even seeing my dad, for crying out loud, because he goes to work before I wake up and he doesn't come home from his three jobs until after midnight. But I'll bet stupid Jimmy's dad gives him a big fat kiss before he walks him to the school bus line in the morning and says something corny, like, "Have a good day, son!" I'd die to have one of my parents say something corny to me like in a movie, but if I ever admitted that to Fay or Bridget or even Nora, they'd laugh in my face and tell me I was an idiot for wanting the impossible.

Seriously, if I'm going to get yelled at by Mrs. Weiss for not being responsible, she should yell at everyone else in this room who have moms who do everything for them, because they probably wouldn't remember any better than I would. It's not fair. But of course I can't say any of this out loud. I think it might be better if I just run out of the room before I cry.

Jordan suddenly stands up from his desk, walks to me, and puts a pencil on my desk without looking at me. He goes back and sits down without a word. Mrs. Weiss looks like she's going to scold Jordan for helping me, but he just stares at her like he did with my sister Fay after church that Sunday. I try to catch his eye to thank him, but he doesn't look my way. Mrs. Weiss finally turns around and tells us to begin.

The thing about being dyslexic is that the more pressure there is on you to read quickly, the faster the letters run around, too. It's exhausting. My eyes feel like they're climbing a mountain. Once I make the words sit still, I'm fine. I know all the answers, but it takes me forever.

I've never taken a test this long before. Usually there are only about ten questions, and I always seem to make it through them, or at least eight or nine, so my grades stay up. But this test has over thirty questions on it. It'll take me all day.

I hear Mrs. Weiss say, "If you've finished and checked your answers, you may bring your tests to me. Then return to your desks and sit quietly until the bell rings."

I look over my shoulder and see that everyone else is done.

The words roll and twist in waves. It's like I'm staring at boiling alphabet soup. The bell rings and Mrs. Weiss says, "Pencils down."

I put my pencil down, but I didn't finish. Why am I so slow? I've had my eyes checked a couple of times, but the truth is I have perfect vision. It's my brain that scrambles everything up. Glasses can't fix someone who's wrong in the head.

Everyone gets up from their seats. I hurry to catch up with Jordan to give him back his pencil.

He shakes his head when I offer it. "Keep it. We've got exams all day," he says, but he still won't look at me.

And all day it's the same. Everyone else in ACT is done long before the bell, but I never finish in time. I can feel them all staring at me, watching me try to read the questions. By the end of the day my head feels like a piece of meat.

The last class is the worst. It's history, and the questions are so long. I sort of give up about halfway through. I just can't stare at the swirling letters anymore. The bell rings and I put my pencil down. Everyone leaves, but I stay in my seat, rubbing my eyes and my temples.

When I get up, I see Jordan's still sitting in his seat, too. He's already turned his test in, so I don't know why he's still here. His leg is bouncing like crazy. He suddenly jumps up and comes to me. He snatches my test off my desk before I can stop him and backs away from me. He starts reading aloud so our history teacher, Mr. Bennet, can hear.

"Annie," Jordan says, "when did the Pilgrims land on Plymouth Rock?" he asks.

"Wh-what?" I stammer, but Jordan snaps at me.

"Just answer the question."

"William Bradford and the *Mayflower* Pilgrims landed in 1620," I say.

Jordan flips the pages on the mimeographed sheets to the back of the test, where I didn't even make it. "Name the original thirteen colonies," he says.

"Delaware, Pennsylvania, Georgia, New Jersey, Connecticut, Maryland, South Carolina, North Carolina, New

Hampshire, Virginia, New York, Providence Plantations, and Massachusetts Bay Colony, of course," I say, ticking each one off on my fingers even though I don't need to. I can count to thirteen, for crying out loud.

Jordan looks at Mr. Bennet. "I missed Pennsylvania," he admits. "Annie knows every single answer in every class. You're testing her all wrong."

He puts my exam papers down on Mr. Bennet's desk and walks out of the room.

Mr. Bennet and I look at each other like neither of us knows what the hell (ten Hail Marys) just happened. Then Mr. Bennet picks up my test and asks me another one of the questions I didn't get to yet.

"What bird did Benjamin Franklin want for our national symbol?" he asks.

I bust out laughing. "The turkey!" I say. "That would have been hilarious." Mr. Bennet laughs, too.

"Correct. But do you know why?" he asks, getting serious.

"Because turkeys are native to North America, and eating them kept the colonists alive when they first got here," I answer. "Ben Franklin was right. The turkey should be on our money, even if it is goofy-looking."

Mr. Bennet smiles and pushes up his glasses. He puts my test away. "I'm going to add those correct answers to your final score," he tells me.

I feel about a hundred pounds lighter. "Thanks, Mr. Bennet. Have a good Christmas," I say.

"You too, Annie," he says, giving me another nice smile.

I hurry out to the bus line, but I don't see Jordan anywhere. He would've waited for me if he wanted to be friends again. I shiver and I realize I left my coat in my locker. It's too late anyways. I barely jump on the bus in time as it is.

It's my fault I left my coat behind. I know that, and I knew my mom was going to get angry about it, but I didn't *know* it at the moment I was running to try to catch up with Jordan. I just wanted to see him, and maybe even get him to smile.

When I get home, I know right away that everything is off. It's not a smell or a taste. You can't see it or hear it, but it's everywhere. When my mother's on her last straw and she's going to lose it, there is never any warning, but you learn to sniff and listen and see and feel something that isn't really ever in your nose, your ears, your eyes, or your hands.

When you're the youngest of nine kids and your mom is stretched so thin you can practically walk through her, you know when to be afraid.

When I get home, I know it. And I'm afraid.

It's her eyes. And then it's her wedding ring and a

pretty flash of every color and then pain—but not in the skin. I mean, yeah, in the skin, but not really.

Pain in the skin is easy to leave behind. Like falling off a bike. Minutes later, and who cares? But when my mother hits me, it hurts the part of me that can't stop asking why, even though I know the answer. She's hitting me because I won't have a warm coat for the entire winter break until school opens again, but I still don't know why she would do it. I can't understand why she would want to hurt me, and that hurts more than the hitting. Not right away, but later. It's like an echo that gets louder the farther away it is because it keeps coming back, and each time it comes back to you it hurts more and more. No matter how hard you push it down, or tell yourself it isn't happening, it is happening. It's happening to me right now and I can't pretend it isn't anymore. I can't pretend it *doesn't* happen anymore.

It's about a coat, but it's not about a coat. It's never about what it's about.

And now I'm not just in trouble. I'm in danger. I can tell by her eyes. Mom's eyes go away and all that's left are flat bird eyes. She's not in there anymore, and that's the part that gives me nightmares. The edges of the world shrink in around me.

"Not Annie," Fay yells from somewhere far away.

I feel myself getting pulled back. Nora and Bridget have me. Fay stands over me.

"Get her out of here," Fay says. And for a second she sounds like she did when we were really little. *She* sounds really little. And then she turns and throws her arms up, using her body to block mine.

Nora and Bridget push me to the door, and then we're outside in the snow with the fat multicolored Christmas lights glowing on the bushes and St. Francis of Assisi is lit red and green and holding a blue stone dove. I want to count. I want to focus on a string of even numbers to calm myself, but I don't because I know it's not going to change anything. And then we're across the street and into the forest and the snow and the silence, and we can't even hear Fay screaming anymore.

There's a beautiful house on the other side of the forest.

It's all glass and thick beams of exposed, stained wood. Its Christmas lights are small and white. A perfectly decorated tree stands in front of the gigantic pane of glass of the living room window. This tree is all red velvet bows and hand-blown glass bulbs. Our tree is a cheap tinsel bomb that's been knocked over three times because Geronimo keeps trying to climb it.

We stare at the tree rather than look at each other. We've hidden in the forest many times before, but this time is especially sad because the Christmas lights are telling us we should be happy, and the Christmas lights are especially cheery here on the country club side of town.

"What if we just kept going?" Nora asks. Bridget and I don't say anything.

After staring at the house and the covered underground pool in the backyard for a while, we go back. We go back because I'm supposed to be Mary in the Nativity play that night. We go back because we're cold and we didn't bring jackets and Nora's only wearing one shoe. But really, we go back because we always go back. We go back because we only have two choices. Stay or run. Both are bad. One is worse, but we don't know which is the worse one yet, so we do what we know to do. Creep in and see how badly Fay is hurt.

We get ice. We flush the bloody toilet paper away. We tell Fay to rinse out her mouth and we make sure she doesn't wiggle her loose teeth. They'll set again if she leaves them alone. We do it all quietly so no one will hear, even though we know no one's listening. Makes me wonder why we're always so quiet about it.

The beatings are the one thing Fay never charges us for or holds over our heads. They're the one thing she never talks about. They're the one thing none of us ever talk about.

Chapter Eight

We get to church and I have to go to the dressing room to put on my costume.

There's a pillow with straps on it that I have to tie around my waist so I look pregnant. Clothes are a challenge for me on a normal day. On a day like today, when I'm all thumbs from the tests and, you know, *Mom*, I can barely figure out how to zip up my own fly, let alone get into this goddamn (like, six rosaries) contraption. I can hear the priests getting antsy outside my changing room.

"Do you need help?" Father Joe asks from the other side of the door.

What's he going to do? Come in here and dress me? "Almost done," I say.

I'm sweating now. I stop looking in the mirror and

let my hands feel what they're supposed to do and finally manage to get into the pillow baby. I throw the white robe on and come out while I'm still putting the blue scarf over my head. The priests and the altar boys and the rest of the cast look relieved. The kid who's playing Joseph (I just found out his name is Peter, because he's from one town over, so I don't know him from school) grabs my hand and drags me out onto the altar because I'm already late.

The lights come up on us. I can't see a damn (ten Hail Marys) thing. Peter says his first line, and I say my first line, and then the lights come down and Father Joe keeps telling the story of us going to be counted in the census while Peter and I and the kid who's playing the donkey go down to the next set, which are the inns. They're in front of the altar, right before the first row of pews.

The kids playing the innkeepers all say they've got no room, and I'm walking next to Peter, trying to look holy, when I see Jordan sitting in the front row with his mom and dad. He smiles at me, and I feel so happy he's looking at me and smiling that I just stand there smiling back at him until Peter kicks me. Peter has to repeat his last line because I've gone totally blank.

I actually say, "Uh . . ." and everyone in the whole church laughs except for Peter.

Then I remember my line and I say, "Oh yeah," and everyone laughs again and I say what I'm supposed to say with a big grin because I'm not embarrassed. Even if I did mess up, I made Jordan Dolan smile, which is like a thousand times better than getting all the lines right in some dumb Nativity play.

And that's as far into the play as we go tonight, because the whole Birth of Jesus bit with the angels and the drummer boy doesn't come until Christmas Eve and that's still a few days away. And Peter's relieved because I don't say anything in the next part. It's all, "Lo and behold," from Angel Number One and the Three Wise Men saying what they've brought for presents, and the kid who plays the drummer boy does this solo drum bit.

After Mass I go to find my family, and my brother, JP, looks at the pillow baby and says, "That's disturbing," which makes Evie and Aurora laugh so hard the three of them have to run outside so they don't get in trouble. Just before JP leaves with Evie and Aurora, he gives me a hug and whispers, "You looked beautiful up there." JP is the only person who's ever told me that.

I feel someone touch my shoulder, and I turn around and there's Jordan.

"Good job," he says.

I make a face. "I forgot one third of my lines," I say back.

"Yeah, but you didn't get nervous or anything."

I shrug because I don't think not getting nervous is enough to make you a good actress.

"Still, with only a two-out-of-three average, I don't think Carl Sagan would approve of me being an actress," I say.

He grins, because he knows exactly what I'm talking about even if we haven't said anything about our destiny in months.

"See you Christmas Eve," he says, giving me a little wave good-bye.

"We'll be here," I say, patting my pillow baby. He shakes his head and goes to his folks.

"Jordan?" I call after him. I take a few steps toward him, and he comes back to meet me halfway. "Sorry about saying no to you in the cafeteria in front of everyone like I did," I say. "That was really mean of me, and I'm sorry."

He's quiet for a while, thinking about exactly how to say what he wants to say. I wait for him to be ready, even though I'm pretty scared about what he might decide. What if he figures he's still angry with me after all?

"I guess we're the kind of friends who do science projects together," he says. "Not the kind who go to dances together."

"But we are friends, right?"

He smiles. "Always," he says.

I realize that the rock was still in my stomach. It never went away until just now. I got so used to it being there I stopped noticing it, but now that it's gone, I feel light and fluttery inside. I also realize I've been holding my breath, and I let it out in a big whooshing sound. I'm so glad that's over.

"Thanks for today," I say before he can walk away.

He nods, because he knows I'm talking about the pencil he lent me and what he did in Mr. Bennet's class and not about how he said I did good in the play or how he forgave me for being mean. Jordan always knows what I'm talking about without me having to go back and explain myself.

I can't stop smiling.

Even though pretty much all of today was awful, at least it ended great. I'm really happy while I go to find Nora so she can come and help me get out of this crappy (five Hail Marys) costume, which is what I should have done when I was putting it on, I realize too late.

"You forgot a line," Nora says as she wrestles me out of my pillow baby. "What could you possibly be so happy about?"

I think about her question for a while, like Jordan would. "I guess I just find different stuff every day," I say.

I find out on Christmas Eve that not only is Miri not

coming back from school to spend Christmas with us, but I'm also going to be stuck sitting in the manger for the entire night. I get bathroom breaks and whatnot, but mostly I have to sit there staring at a baby doll while three separate masses happen.

I get why Miri doesn't want to come home, but if Father Joe had told me that I was going to have to do the whole play, then sit up on the altar in the manger with Peter and the kid who's playing the donkey (his name's Bobby, and he's from the same town as Peter) for the five o'clock, the seven o'clock, and the nine o'clock masses, I never would have agreed to it. We always spend most of Christmas at church, but this is too much, even for me.

Jordan and his parents show up for the seven o'clock Mass, so at least I can look forward to talking to him at the end of it. Sure enough, when Mass is done, Jordan comes and finds me.

"You were great. You didn't mess up any of your lines this time," he says, smiling.

"Ha-ha," I say because, duh, I didn't have any lines.

"But I think the donkey fell asleep."

"Yeah, but it doesn't matter because he's a donkey," I say. "Anyways, he's only eight, so he doesn't have to do the nine o'clock with us."

"You're here for another Mass?" Jordan looks surprised in a way that actually makes me feel better.

I nod. "Christmas takes too long."

Jordan's parents come up behind him. "Jordan, are you almost ready to leave?" his father asks.

Jordan turns to me. "What do you do in between masses?" he asks.

I shrug. "Not much," I say. "Between the five and seven I melted down three altar candles and made a snowman and an angel out of the drippings. Wanna see where I burned my hand catching the hot wax?"

I show him the red mark on my palm. It's over my Jesus Hole, but bigger.

"Awesome," Jordan says. "Did it hurt?"

"Only for a second, and then it starts to cool and then you can make, like, anything out of it."

Jordan turns back to his parents. "Can I hang out here with Annie?" he asks.

His parents look at each other. "Don't you want to get home and open your Christmas Eve present?" his mom asks.

"I'd rather stay with Annie," Jordan says.

His parents look at each other again, and for a second it's like neither of them knows what to do.

"I think we'd better go, Jordan," his father says. "It's getting late. We'll watch a movie when we get home."

"Fine," Jordan says, sighing. He looks back at me. "I guess I'll see you next year."

"Have a good Christmas," I say.

I include his parents when I say it, but they don't smile at me. His mom especially. She's looking at me like I tried to steal gum out of her purse. Not that Jordan's mom looks like she chews gum. In fact, she's the kind of person who'd probably say gum chewing is vulgar. I like gum, not that my parents ever let me have it. My dad thinks it's vulgar.

I'm so tired when I finally get home. My big sisters and my brother are in the playroom watching *A Christmas Carol*—the creepy one with George C. Scott. They've got blankets all over the place, and everyone's in a heap on the floor next to the Christmas tree. I scoot in between Aurora and JP, and Geronimo growls at me from under the covers and I have to scoot around him so he doesn't take a swipe at me. I don't even care that I can't see the TV, because I fall asleep in like two seconds.

I feel like I'm floating and open my eyes just a smidge. JP is carrying me up the stairs. I close my eyes and pretend to be asleep so he doesn't put me down, but he isn't fooled. After he tucks me into the top bunk, he says, "Merry Christmas, Annie."

I smile even though I'm trying not to. I love it when JP carries me to bed and tucks me in. It's the only time I ever sleep without any nightmares at all.

Christmas morning at 17 Snow Lane is nothing like it is in the movies. In the movies there's always snow falling and kids in pajamas running downstairs to rip open their giant presents and the fake mom and dad are smiling and happy and the kids believe in Santa. At 17 Snow Lane, there's usually snow on the ground at Christmas, but it's always just patches of the old, melted kind with brown leaves everywhere in between. We don't get to open our presents first thing in the morning. Oh, no. We have to wait until after Mass, and my parents aren't even there when we wake up because they're already at church, and we've never believed in Santa because he's pagan.

Nora and I find some fruitcake to eat and share a glass of milk, because that's all that's left in the fridge, while we wait for our turn in the bathroom. We go back upstairs, sing "Fool in the Rain" (I actually really like this one because of the whistle and fast bit in the middle that feels like a party), and get dressed, and then we have to chase Geronimo out of the Christmas tree before we all pile into the van and head back to church.

When Mass is over, we go back home and wait for the Italians to show up with the lasagna. My aunt always makes an industrial-size pan of lasagna for Christmas and Easter, and we get to eat as much as we want. By the time the relatives show up and the lasagna's eaten and we're ready to open presents, it's usually about four o'clock in the afternoon.

The waiting used to be torture, but once I realized that I never get anything good anyway, it got much easier.

I'm the Elf this year. That means I have to dive into the pile of presents, read off the name, and then throw the gift to the person it's for. I like being the Elf, even if it means I have to wait until the last present is given out to open my own. I keep calling out names and chucking presents, and a bunch of times I see Nora's face looking hopeful, but the presents are always for someone else. I'm down to the last few presents when I realize she doesn't have any.

Mom forgot Nora.

I check the last few name tags to make sure, but it's no use. Nora didn't get any presents this year. The Italians gave her money (they always give us twenty bucks for Christmas), but that's it. That's all Nora got.

I go and sit next to her. She's looking pale and woozy.

"You can have half of mine," I tell her, but she shakes her head. I know what she means. It's not what's in them that matters. It's getting them, and she didn't get anything for Christmas.

I see Fay and Bridget and the big piles in front of them. Fay got a Cabbage Patch doll, which is, like, *whoa*. They're so hard to get, it was even on the news and everything how people had to stand in line for hours to get them and even grown-ups were buying them for themselves because they are collector's items. Everyone wants one. You'd think with her getting a Cabbage Patch doll and everything, Fay would be running around screaming, but instead she keeps looking at Nora.

I shove some of my presents in front of Nora and whisper, "Just help me open them, okay?"

Nora's face is totally blank, like, blanker than Jordan's when he clams up. She helps me unwrap my crappy (five Hail Marys) tube socks and ugly shirts and old-lady Isotoner gloves that I'll never *ever* wear even if it's a thousand degrees below zero out, but she's not really here next to me.

Chapter Nine

The whole school is finally excited about Christa McAuliffe.

Today is the launch of the space shuttle *Challenger*, and the teachers aren't going to be teaching, so we can all watch on TVs that they've wheeled into every single classroom. They've even opened all the doors between the classrooms so we can watch with whoever we like, too.

The only time they've ever canceled classes before was because of a blizzard, and I've never seen them open all the doors. This is the biggest deal in my school ever.

Jordan brought the new Walkman he got last month for Christmas into school today so we could share his headphones and listen in, just in case. Which turned out to be a great idea because everyone is running around and making so much racket Jordan and I can't hear the TV. We sit in the back of the science classroom under the table with the hamster on it while Jordan searches the radio.

"Doesn't Wilson ever get tired of making fart noises?" I ask Jordan as Wilson runs by with a hand in his armpit.

"It's all he's got," he replies.

"And you know he won't even wash that hand before he eats lunch."

"No point." Jordan grins. "He's just going to stick his hand back in his armpit to make fart noises while he's eating."

I laugh because it's gross and true.

Jordan suddenly looks down at his Walkman. "I found it," he says, and slips off his earphones so he can pull out the metal extenders.

Even with the extenders all the way out, we still have to press ourselves together so we can fit the earphones over both our heads, but I don't mind being this close to Jordan. He always smells like dryer sheets and Ivory soap, and his breath doesn't smell like much of anything at all. Maybe a little like fruit punch, because that's his favorite drink.

We listen to the broadcaster telling us about the astronauts and the training they went through and how hard they had to study and stuff. I can feel Jordan getting more and more excited.

"I want to be an astronaut," he says quietly.

I turn a little bit toward him so I can see his eyes out of the corner of mine. "Jordan? Do you think that's your destiny?"

He looks down and runs his thumb over the stenciling on his Walkman, like he's embarrassed to say it out loud.

"I bet you'll walk on Mars," I whisper. His face lights up.

"Come with me," he says. "We'll walk on Mars together."

I smile because I think I'd love to go to Mars with Jordan, but it makes me sad, too, because no matter how much fun that would be, I don't think being an astronaut is my destiny.

Jordan can tell my smile isn't a real smile, and he's just about to make me tell him why when great clouds of smoke and water vapor start shooting out from under the space shuttle *Challenger* on TV.

"It's starting," Jordan says, and we both stand up.

Mr. Bennet cranks up the volume on the TV and we all crowd around it, doing the countdown with the flight coordinator at Cape Canaveral. *Three, two, one . . . and, liftoff!*

The whole school is cheering. *Challenger* shoots into the sky in a huge cloud of steam and fire and ice. I grow two feet probably, my heart is lifting me up so high. Jordan grabs my hand. I can feel every bit of him squeezing, like he needs to hold on to me so he doesn't grow wings and fly away. *Challenger* rolls and climbs higher and higher.

And then

An orange flash and a white cloud are all that's left. It's gone. It's just . . . gone.

"No," I hear Jordan say.

The one big cloud of white breaks off into two separate trails. One of them is still burning. It feels like everything is going slow.

"No," Jordan says again, even louder.

Mr. Bennet drops his head into his hands and starts crying. I've never seen a teacher cry before. I can't even breathe.

I look at Jordan. He looks at me. I can't imagine if Jordan turned into a puff of white smoke. Even thinking it is too hard. How can those people who were just smiling and waving and rising into the sky be dead?

"I don't want you to be an astronaut," I tell him. "Promise me you won't."

He's still holding my hand because I won't let him

let go. After a while he nods. "Okay, Annie," he says. "I promise."

The rest of the day is not like school at all. Jordan and I sit under the hamster table and listen to the reports on his Walkman with our heads pressed together. Nobody has any answers. NASA is launching an investigation. It doesn't matter how many times we listen to the same thing over and over. It still doesn't seem real.

After a while, Jordan takes the headphones off us.

"Was that their destiny?" he asks me. I don't like the look in his eyes. It's mean. It reminds me of Fay.

"No," I say. "No, that was an accident."

"So their destiny was an accident?"

"What are you talking about?" I ask, because I'm really confused now.

"When those seven astronauts got on that shuttle, everyone thought it was their destiny," he says. His eyes are narrow and he's clenching his jaw. "So was it? Were they wrong, or was it their destiny to die?"

Now I'm angry, because he's starting to sound like Nora and Fay and everyone else in my family who spends more time thinking about everything that's broken rather than thinking about how to make anything better. I don't want Jordan to be like my family.

"It was their destiny to *try*," I say. I butt-scoot out

from under the hamster table. When I get out, I turn around and look at Jordan, and even though we just spent months in a huge fight, this is the first time I've ever actually yelled at him. "It was their destiny to want to do something important with their lives. Just because it didn't work doesn't mean it didn't mean anything."

I leave the room, but I have no idea where I'm going. That's the problem with yelling at your best friend. You're sort of left with nothing to do afterward.

I wander the halls and end up in the ACT room. I start taking materials out of the tool cabinet. I miss building things. I especially want to build something now that I've seen something blow up. But Jordan's the builder. I can't measure right or use a drill. I'm just the idea girl.

There's all this copper wire and a bunch of magnets in the drawer from the Faraday experiment Jordan and I did last year. I take out the copper wire and start thinking.

"We're not allowed to do anything with an electrical current this year, remember?" Jordan says behind me.

I turn around and face him. "Because of your mom." I grimace at him. "I only electrocuted you a little bit, and it was your project to begin with."

"Yeah, I know," he says. "She just likes to blame other people for stuff I do wrong." He comes all the way into the room and starts taking materials out of the cabinet with me.

"So what were you thinking of making?" he asks.

I shrug. I'm trying to picture it. I want to build something that is the exact opposite of the space shuttle blowing up.

"I don't know," I say. "Something with light."

Jordan nods. "Prisms?" he guesses.

Now I know he's on board no matter what I say. Mostly, I think he just needs something to look forward to again. Maybe that's why I'm doing it, because I know Jordan, and I know that he needs something to build.

"I heard about this experiment where you can make a flashlight out of paper and graphite," I say.

Jordan smiles. "Does it use electricity?"

"Probably." I smile back. "Your mom doesn't *have* to know about it, you know."

"Describe it," he says. He goes to the chalkboard to start writing down what I say.

We only come up with ideas for how we're going to build it, and we don't actually start working on the flashlight just yet because we need to do more research, but I don't care that we don't start today. It's enough that we have a project to work on together.

When the final bell rings, Jordan and I walk to the bus lines together.

"Sorry about your destiny," I say. "You'll find another one, though."

He looks at the floor as we walk and doesn't say anything for a while. "How do you know that?" he asks.

"Because you're good at everything," I say, rolling my eyes in just the right way to make him laugh. "It'll probably take me until I'm eighty, because there's pretty much nothing I'm good at."

Jordan frowns at me, like what I said made him angry. "You're good at making people feel better."

"That's not a destiny, Jordan. It's not *important*."

He stops walking and I have to stop with him. "It is to me," he says.

We don't say anything while we walk the rest of the way to our buses, because we don't need to.

When I get home, my mom tells us she "found" a bag of presents from Christmas she forgot to give us.

My mom does this every year. She hides one bag of presents so she can surprise us all when winter is dragging on and no one has anything to look forward to because spring is still ages away. And it works, actually. It makes a crap (five Hail Marys) day like today with the shuttle disaster actually bearable. See, my mom does really try, and in a way I always wonder how great a mom she would have been if she'd been able to do it her way. Maybe she still wouldn't have been perfect, but it's things like the bags full of "forgotten" gifts that make me think she could have been good at it if there had only been two or three of us. We'd have had more money, too.

I said that to Nora once, and she said, "Yeah, but that would mean you and I wouldn't be here."

I've mentioned this before, because it's something I think about a lot, but not in a sad way. I don't get why it's so terrible to think things would have been better if you'd never been born, but I know enough not to say that in front of anyone but Nora, because they'd think I was depressed or something. I just don't think it's so awful to imagine not being born. It's way better than imagining hell, and they make me do that all the time at church.

Mom hands Nora and me our gifts with a big smile when we walk in the door from school.

I got a pair of work gloves. "You know, for your projects at school," my mom says.

"Thanks," I say, slightly confused. "They're . . . perfect, actually."

Sometimes my mom really does get me, and it's times like this that I wonder when she's looked at me enough to notice these things about me. Maybe she's got another pair of eyes.

I'm so happy with my work gloves (which actually fit)

that I'm smiling when I look over at Nora. She's opened her gift and is looking at it with a frown. It's a dress for a Cabbage Patch doll.

"What's this for?" she asks Mom.

"It's for the Cabbage Patch doll I got you for Christmas," Mom says.

"You gave Fay the doll," Nora says, handing the dress back to Mom. Mom won't take it.

"No. I got *you* the Cabbage Patch doll," Mom insists. "Didn't you notice how she has your eyes and hair color? I waited in line for three hours to get you that doll. Don't tell me you've lost her, Eleanor."

Now, here's the thing about my mom. I've mentioned that she's forgetful, but that doesn't really explain it. She's the most absentminded person ever. She's left me behind at the grocery store, she's forgotten to pick me up after doctors' appointments for, like, hours, and she's even forgotten my name and stared at me, snapping her fingers for five solid minutes, while she tried to remember who the heck I am. She's the most forgetful person ever. And she never forgets anything.

Okay, now I know it seems impossible for her to be both, but trust me, she is. Things slip my mom's mind all the time, but she remembers everything exactly the way it happened. I think I get my memory from her, now that I think of it, because I'm the same way. But that's not important right now. What's important is that Nora is turning red. Her hand is clamped around the dress, and it looks like she's about to throw a fit.

She turns away from Mom and runs up the steps. I run along behind her because I'm worried about her. Nora throws open the door to Bridget and Fay's room and catches them trying to hide the Cabbage Patch doll.

"You took my name off all my presents and put your own names on them, didn't you?" Nora asks.

Fay lies a lot. She cheats all the time. If you catch her in a lie, she weasels out of it. But not even Fay can lie her way out of the doll she's trying to hide. She looks embarrassed for a second, and then she throws the doll at Nora so hard it bounces off her and falls on the floor.

"You can have it," Fay says. "It's just a stupid doll."

Nora bends down and picks up the Cabbage Patch doll. She leaves the room without saying another word. I follow her.

Nora's on her bed, changing her doll into the new dress Mom bought. Her doll has a scuff mark on her face, and her yarn hair is all ratty. Fay wasn't nice to this doll at all.

"I bet you can get that scuff mark out," I say.

Nora's crying silently. She smooths the dress and won't even look at me. Sometimes I wish Nora would just let me be her sister, but she won't.

Chapter Ten

I've been going on my sisters' dates with them since I was six.

Mom's rule is: if you want to go on a date with a Bianchi girl, Annie goes, too. So if a boy wants to take one of my sisters to a movie, it has to be one I'm old enough to see, and I'm supposed to sit between the two of them the whole time. If a boy wants to take one of my sisters driving, I'm riding in the backseat. And my bedtime is ten o'clock, so that's when the date's over.

I've been on a lot of dates, but I still have no idea how some of my sisters end up liking the boys they like. My sister Aurora, especially.

Aurora gets asked out every weekend, and there have been some really great boys who've even bought me popcorn *and* candy, which is, like, super nice. There have been boys who've told Aurora she was beautiful and asked her to wear their letterman jackets, but they've never gotten more than two dates.

The *really* polite boys who try to talk to her about ballet and her career never even get a second date. They dress nice, drive fancy cars, and have money. I can tell Aurora is nervous around them. The guys Aurora always ends up going out on more dates with are duds.

Take Stan, for instance.

Stan, Aurora, and I have gone on four dates now, and I have no idea why my sister keeps going out with this guy. He's got a crap (five Hail Marys) car. He never buys any popcorn. He starts the night out really charming and funny, but by the end of the date, he always ends up yelling at Aurora for something and they start fighting, and not just arguing back and forth in a funny way, like Evangeline always does with her boyfriend, Patrick. I mean, Stan and Aurora *fight*. Usually about something that didn't even happen. Like the time Stan said that Aurora was flirting with the guy who took her movie ticket. Aurora didn't even say hi to him, though, so I have no idea what Stan was talking about.

Stan is the worst. And we're going out with him again tonight. When he picks up Aurora and me, he gives me this look, like he can't believe I'm here.

"I thought you were going to ditch her," Stan says.

Aurora shakes her head. "You know the rules," she says.

"But your sister Evie and Patrick can go out alone," he says.

Yeah, because my parents like Patrick and you're a jerk, I think, but I keep my mouth shut. I know when to keep quiet on my sisters' dates.

"Patrick and Evie have been dating since she was thirteen," Aurora says. She puts a hand on my shoulder and stops me before we get in the car. "If you don't like it, Annie and I can go back inside."

Please say you don't like it, Stan.

"It's fine," he says, even though I can tell it isn't.

"Get in the car, Littlebit," she tells me. Ugh. I really don't want to, but I do what she says.

We get in his ugly, smelly car and go to the mall. The only movie playing right now that I can go to is *Legend* with Tom Cruise, because it's got unicorns and fairies in it.

I love it. There's glitter on everything and a really pretty girl in a white dress, and summer turns into winter because she touches a unicorn and gets it killed. I almost started crying at that part, but I was too scared because of the goblins, but the girl goes to save the unicorns and she has to face the devil. He turns her white dress black and comes out of a mirror with his hooves and horns. He's got this cape on and it blows all around him and he's so cool and I think I love the devil now. (Ten *thousand* rosaries, probably.)

I'm so wrapped up in the movie that I barely even notice Stan feeling up my sister.

After the movie, Stan keeps talking about how stupid it was, and I wonder how he even knows what happened, seeing as how he spent half the time trying to get his hand up Aurora's skirt. With me in between them. Like I said, Stan is the worst.

"That was the dumbest movie I've ever seen," Stan says.

"I liked it," I say. "The unicorns were so pretty."

Stan smirks at me and tries to pull Aurora away and take her around behind the Cineplex. "She'll be all right on her own for a minute," he says to my sister.

"We can't just leave her," Aurora says.

"Come *on*," Stan says. He grabs her wrist real hard and starts to drag her. I follow them away from the lights out front and through the bushes and around the corner, because I don't like how scared Aurora looks.

"Go back to the front of the movie theater, Annie," my sister says. "I'll come and get you soon."

"Let's just go home, Aurora. Please?" I beg.

"Shut up, Annie," Stan yells at me.

"Don't talk to my baby sister like that," Aurora says

back, and Stan slaps her. She shoves him and he slaps her again, so hard she falls down.

I'm frozen. I know I should help my sister up, but I feel like I'm stuck and, if I stay really still, this won't be happening. Stan paces around in a circle.

"See what you made me do?" he says. "Why didn't you just come around back with me?" he yells at my sister, and it looks like he's going to hit her again. Then it's like I switch on again, even if it is too late.

"No!" I shout. "Get away from her."

"Shh, kid, shut your mouth," Stan growls at me.

I back away from him. "Don't hit my sister!" I scream. People are starting to look around the corner.

"Get Annie to shut her mouth," Stan says, real quiet, to my sister.

Aurora stands up and grabs me. "It's okay, Annie," she says, but it's not okay. The left side of her face is all red, and blood is smeared on her bottom lip. She turns to Stan. "Take us home," she says.

"Get yourself home, whore," he says. And then Stan's gone.

It's a long walk back home. I mean, miles. I count license plates, and the weird thing is that they're all divisible by three and fit perfectly into three separate sets and everything should be okay, but it isn't.

I hear Aurora crying. She's the only one of us who

makes any sound when she cries, but since everything Aurora does is pretty, she sounds like a dove when she does it. We have to stop and sit so I can rest. Aurora doesn't need to rest. She may look fragile, but she's as strong as an ox from so many years of ballet. Aurora could probably run to Boston and back without getting tired.

We're sitting on a rock right on the edge of the forest. We'll cut through and get home maybe half an hour sooner once I rest my legs a little. It's way past my bedtime. Aurora's done crying now but she's even more sad, somehow.

"Why don't you go out with the guys who are nice to you?" I ask her. "They buy popcorn and tell you you're pretty."

She sighs like I don't know what I'm talking about. "You think they're better?" she asks.

"Yes," I say, but she shakes her head.

"No, Annie. Those boys are even worse. They don't call me a whore just because they're angry, but they think it all the time."

"But you're not," I say.

She smiles at me. "It doesn't matter what I am. It matters what they think I am, because that's how they treat me."

"But the nice guys wouldn't hit you," I say, like it's

obvious. I try to think of the nicest boys she's dated. "Shane Thomson. He'd never hit you."

"Maybe not, Littlebit," she says. She smooths my frizzy hair. Her hair still looks like black ice. "But I don't want Shane."

"Why not?" I ask, like she's a crazy person. "He's *so* nice. And remember how he made you laugh so hard Diet Coke came out your nose?"

She looks down at her hands. "Shane's nice. He's from a good family. He'd never understand—"

I wait for her to finish, but then I realize she isn't going to. "Never understand what?" I ask.

She shrugs and won't look at me. "He's not right for me." She looks ashamed. "Actually, I'm not right for him. We're going to graduate in one month, and then he's off to Harvard. He's a legacy." I have no idea what that means, but I think it's important. Aurora points at the bruise darkening her face. "Do you think I'd fit in with all those rich kids at Harvard?"

"No," I say. "Because you're probably way prettier and more talented than all of them put together."

Aurora laughs. "Oh, Annie." She looks up at the stars, smiling. "I hope you never change."

We cut through the forest, past that beautiful house that's all wood and glass, and we get home after midnight. We have to sneak in, but that's not so hard in my house.

You see, with nine people to account for, Mom and Dad miss half of us in the shuffle. In fact, sometimes they lose track of us even when we're standing right in front of them, like that time Mom ran over Fay's foot with the car on accident. At least, I'm pretty sure it was an accident. Anyways, I can go days without ever even seeing my parents, let alone them getting worried I haven't gone to bed. We walk right in the front door because it's never locked. There's nothing to steal, anyways.

"Don't say anything to JP," Aurora whispers.

"What about your face?" I whisper back. "You're purple."

Aurora touches her cheek. "I'll say Peach dropped me doing a lift."

Peach is Aurora's dance partner. His name is really Pedro, but everyone calls him Peach because he's that sweet. He's even sweeter than Shane, but my sister says she can't date him either because he doesn't date girls, even though he spends all his time with the most beautiful girls in the world. Kind of like JP, actually. JP's got tons of girlfriends, but he doesn't have *a* girlfriend and I don't think he ever has. Huh. I just noticed that. But that's not important right now.

"Everyone knows you weren't dancing tonight," I whisper back frantically. "You can't blame Peach."

We hear someone coming down the stairs and stop talking.

"Do you have any idea what time it is?" Nora says from the bottom of the steps. She folds her arms across her skinny chest and gives Aurora a scolding look. "You can't keep Annie up this late. She'll get sick."

"Be quiet, Nora," Aurora hisses. She rushes forward to drag Nora and me away from the bottom of the steps so our parents don't hear.

My mom can hear an ant fart, especially at night, when her super-hearing is extra looking for any kind of funny business. If you even get up to pee in the middle of the night and put a foot down too hard, you can bet two seconds later Mom's gonna blind you with her flashlight while you're sitting on the toilet. There's nothing worse than having the pee scared back inside you by Mom shining a light in your eyes while you've got your underpants down. She's probably startled five or six years off the end of my life as it is, and I'm the quietest when I get up to pee. Considering it's three of us all talking at the bottom of the stairs, I can't believe Mom isn't down here already, actually.

Aurora drags us into the sewing room/study.

"What happened to your face?" Nora asks. She's sneering when she says it, too.

See, here's the thing about Nora. She's sort of like

Jimmy Collins. They make other people *want* to hurt them.

It's like this. Nora and Jimmy think people are mean, and it's *because* they think that way that other people act mean around them. Jimmy knows he's doing it, and he likes making people act mean and stupid. Nora has no idea, but other people don't know that. They just think she thinks she's better than them, but she doesn't. She's just seen the worst in people so many times she assumes she'll see it again. And nobody likes to be thought of at their worst.

Aurora grabs a big hunk of Nora's hair and twists it until Nora crumples down on her knees.

"You're not going to say anything about this to anyone. Are you, Eleanor?" Aurora whispers.

She looks at Nora with so much hate I can't stand it. It's like Nora is to blame for what happened tonight because she's sneering at Aurora just like all those girls at Harvard would sneer, but Nora isn't to blame for any of it. And Nora knows it, so she just sneers even more at Aurora and stares at Aurora's black eye like she's trash because she has a black eye. But Aurora isn't trash, and *that's* why she has a black eye to begin with, and I wish I could explain this to both of them, but neither of them would believe it because they both think the opposite is true.

I put my hand on top of Aurora's to get her to loosen her grip on Nora as I try to wiggle between my two sisters.

"Nora's not going to say anything," I tell Aurora. "Let go. I swear she won't say anything."

"She better not, the little snitch," Aurora says. I get myself between them.

"She won't tell," I promise. "You should put some ice on your eye, Aurora," I say, and I hustle Nora to the stairs.

Nora feels like dandelion fluff in my arms, she's so light.

"Everyone hates me," she whispers as we tiptoe up the stairs.

We get into our room and I climb into bed without even taking off my clothes first.

"I don't hate you. I love you," I tell her.

She doesn't say she loves me back, but it's okay. Nora never says she loves me, because she can't say it to anyone, or else it's like saying it to no one. She's got to save it all up and only give it away once or it's not special. Maybe she'll finally say it to me when I'm eighty and about to die. But I know she loves me anyway. Nora loves me even though she wishes she didn't.

When I wake up the next morning, Nora's gone.

I know something's wrong right away. Little things

are missing, like Nora's favorite book and the drops she has to put in her ears so she doesn't get any more ear infections. Geronimo sits in the middle of her bed, blinking at me. Almost like he's sad.

I go downstairs without even trying to sing Led Zeppelin to get into the bathroom, and I ask Mom where Nora is.

"She hasn't come down yet," Mom says, and that's when I get really nervous.

"She's not upstairs," I tell Mom, but she doesn't look worried. "Mom. She's not in her bed, and her favorite stuff is gone," I say louder.

Mom sighs and turns to face me. "What do you want me to do, Annie?"

I stand there for a second, because the last time Mom really looked at me was way back when I asked her why she didn't put me in ballet. When I don't have anything to say, Mom goes back to microwaving a bowl of oatmeal for me.

That's when I realize that no one is going to do anything. Nora ran away from home and no one cares.

I eat my oatmeal and wait for Mom to go to church for choir practice before I make a couple of peanut butter and jelly sandwiches for Nora and me. She'll be hungry when I find her, probably. I remember an old thermos in an old lunch box and pour milk into it, put everything into a backpack, and head out into the woods.

It's spring, but it's still not all that warm yet, so I wear JP's old jean jacket over my T-shirt that says VIRGINIA IS FOR LOVERS. I love this T-shirt because it's supersoft, but I hate it, too, because the word *lovers* on it always seems so corny to me, and there's a silhouette of a boy and a girl kissing silk-screened onto it, so I never wear it to school. Plus, I've never been to Virginia, so I hardly ever wear it even if it does feel just right when I put it on, but I need to be comfortable if I'm going to find Nora and convince her to come back, and this T-shirt hugs close and fits great under a jean jacket.

You've got to be wearing just the right things if you're going to be going through the whole woods to rescue your sister.

I start on our usual paths. There are places we like to go and play, like the Witch Cottage, which is really just a tumbledown old house that was made of the same stones the fences are made out of and has probably been here since there were witches running around here after the Salem witch trials. There's no roof or anything, just stone on top of stone to show you where the rooms used to be and piles and piles of dead leaves from years before. Nora's not at the Witch Cottage, so I go on to the Prudential Tree.

The Prudential Tree doesn't have a name on any of the maps, but it has a name with all us kids. It's this old, gnarly pine tree that sticks out over the edge of a cliff. It's huge. I mean, enormous.

The Prue Tree is so wide around the bottom that all eight of my siblings and I can barely hold hands around it. It's so tall that if you climb up even three-quarters of the way, you can see all twenty-six miles into Boston and it's like you're looking directly into the windows of the Prudential Building. That's why we named it the Prue Tree.

It's the best. I've only climbed it once, though, on account of the fact that I pretty much fell out of it and would have died if it hadn't been for Fay.

I was staring at Boston and it looked like a city in one of those snow globes, but without the snow. It was like I could reach out and grab the shining glass and steel and turn it around in my hands.

And then the wind blew and the Prue Tree started swaying back and forth and Patrick (my sister Evangeline's boyfriend, who's been around so long I can't really remember a time without him) started yelling for everyone to look out and, before I knew it, I was falling.

I whooshed past Patrick, and I saw the panic on his face as he tried to grab me, but it was Fay, who was a few branches below him, who managed to get a hand around me, and she saved me. She grabbed me wicked hard, and the branches whipped her and me like crazy as we both fell, but she didn't let go. JP grabbed her as she went by and managed to stop both of us.

I've never been allowed back up since, because everyone says I'm so skinny the wind can just blow me out like a kite and it isn't safe.

But I go there to find Nora.

She's been here. I can see where she sat with her back against the tree and where she scuffed her feet and drew little circles in the ground with a stick because she was bored. And I know it was Nora, because no one knows about the Prue Tree but us Bianchis. And Patrick, but he's one of us anyways now, even if he and Evie aren't quite married yet.

There's no trail. I mean, not that I could spot a trail or anything. I'm practically through to the other side of the forest at this point, so I decide to stop and eat a sandwich. I drink all the milk, too, because it's going warm anyways.

When I'm done with my lunch, I decide to go around the outside of the woods on the nice side of town by the country club to try and see if Nora left the woods or if she stayed inside. I end up at the beautiful house that's all wood and glass.

When I break through the whip-green branches,

I see a sailboat on blocks in the backyard. The boat is raw wooden planks and pegs, handmade, and it's not that big. The hull is up on sawhorses, but I know whose boat this is just from the look of the build. I know a Jordan Dolan project when I see one.

There are no big leaves on the trees yet to hide me, so as soon as I see Jordan and his father, they see me.

"Annie?" Jordan says, like he can't believe I'm here.

I have to come out of the woods and into their yard, but I don't want to.

This is Jordan's house. *This* house, out of every house, is his. And it makes me feel bad. I always knew Jordan and I were different, but knowing he lives here is worse somehow. He's even farther away from me than Kristin Gates, and I'd always hoped maybe he was closer.

I'm barely out of the woods and he runs to meet me. He's excited. He grabs my hand and pulls me toward his boat.

"I've wanted to ask you to come and see my boat forever now," he says, and his voice cracks, going up and down all crazy when he says *forever*. He's breathless and his cheeks are pink. "What are you doing here?"

I smile and stand in front of his boat. "It's beautiful," I say, because it is. It curves and bends and flows, and I can tell just by looking at it that it floats. I turn to Jordan. "It's the best thing you've ever built."

He looks down. "I had so much trouble with the keel," he tells me. He's still holding my hand, so he guides me under the sawhorses so I can see what he means. "I couldn't get it plumb."

I start to laugh because of our pendulum project. We just couldn't get it plumb, which was hilarious for five seconds because I said we should just paint it purple, but then it turned into a giant pain that I never figured out, but Jordan did because he always figures everything out.

"It looks plumb now," I say. I glance at Jordan out of the corner of my eye. "And you didn't even have to paint it."

Jordan and I laugh because we both know exactly what we're talking about.

"Jordan's worked very hard on this," his dad says. He's standing outside because he's too big to fit underneath.

Jordan and I come out from under the boat. His dad looks at our hands because we're still holding them. My cheeks get hot and I twist my hand out of Jordan's.

Nobody says anything for a while, and I know how much Jordan hates that. It's not that Jordan doesn't like to talk, it's that he never knows what to say when he thinks other people won't understand him. Now that I see him with his dad, I get why he's like that, but I still don't know what to do. Normally, I'd do the talking for Jordan, but I don't know how to do that with his dad here.

"You're Annie, right?" his father asks.

I nod.

"You're growing up," he says.

"I turned eleven," I say.

"Do you live on this side of town?"

"No," I say. "I live on Snow Lane."

"That's a long walk," Mr. Dolan says.

I nod again.

Jordan shifts from foot to foot. It's what he does instead of bouncing his leg when he's standing up and not sitting down. I hate it when Jordan's uncomfortable.

"I gotta go," I say. I start backing toward the woods.

"Why?" Jordan asks.

"I gotta find my sister," I say.

Jordan frowns. He comes forward and takes my arm so I can't melt away into the trees. His eyes drop and he looks at my T-shirt, and I can tell he likes it because he stares at the silk screen on my chest for a really long time. He moves closer to me.

"Which sister?" he asks. There's sun on his hair, and he has to tilt his chin down to look me in the eye. When did Jordan Dolan get taller than me?

"The closest one. Eleanor." I stop and shift my backpack, but really I shrug his hand off. Not because I want to, but because his dad keeps staring at us. He doesn't like that Jordan's touching me.

"What happened?" Jordan asks.

I look at his dad, who's watching us carefully. I can't tell Jordan the truth. I know what his dad will think of my family because Nora ran away.

"I'll tell you Monday," I say, and I run. I stop just before the tree line and turn. "I love your boat," I shout. Then I'm gone.

I don't find Nora. She doesn't come home that night. It takes until Sunday night for my parents to start worrying, even though I've been sick to my stomach about her for over a day now.

And when they start asking about where she might have gone, it's not like it is in the movies. It's not like they tear out their hair and yell at the police with tears in their eyes. At this point, I'm surprised they even called the police. Our family looks normal and nice enough on the outside, and we all try hard to keep it that way. Having the police at your house definitely doesn't look nice.

My parents look tired and they shrug a lot and they ask Officer Langmeyer, "Where could she possibly go besides a friend's house?" like it's no big deal.

But Nora doesn't have any friends. And she isn't at anybody's house.

Chapter Eleven

Monday morning, and Mom makes me go to school. I feel naked sitting on the bus without Nora. Kristin Gates comes and sits next to me as soon as she gets on the bus.

"Is Nora sick?" she asks, worried.

I shake my head, because my heart's pounding and I think I might barf.

"Where is she?" Kristin asks.

I shrug. "We don't know," I say.

I tell Kristin about my parents finally calling the police last night and how we haven't heard anything from them yet. Kristin holds my hand when we walk into school, and it helps a lot.

"Don't worry, Annie. Nora's smart. She's going to be okay until they find her," Kristin says.

When we get to Mrs. Weiss's class, Jordan smiles when he sees me, and then he really sees me, and his smile disappears. He turns around to talk to me as I sit down behind him.

"You didn't find Nora, did you?" he asks.

I shake my head and press my lips together so I don't cry. Jordan starts breathing hard, and his face is clammed up.

"I'll help you look for her after school today in the woods," he says.

I nod so he'll turn around and stop looking at me like that, because I don't think I can handle Jordan looking at me and thinking whatever it is he's thinking, which could be anything, really, because I can't tell when his face is all clammed up.

He turns around, but he reaches back with one of his hands under the desk and finds my leg. Jordan squeezes my calf, and I feel myself start to calm down.

I don't talk all day in school, and that's definitely a first. It's not like I decide not to talk, it's just I can't seem to keep my brain in the same place as my body. At lunch Samantha Schnabel asks what's wrong with me, and Kristin makes up some excuse without telling anyone about my sister, because without me even saying anything she knows I don't want anyone else to know.

Jordan walks with Kristin and me to every class, and

I think he's supposed to have baseball practice after school, but he meets me at the line for the bus anyways. He comes and stands in my line, and then I realize that he's planning on coming home with me.

"We should start on your side of town," I say, panicking.

Jordan frowns. "Why?"

"Because I've checked my side over and over. And I know she's been as far as the Prue Tree, which is nearly to your side of town," I say, coming up with an excuse as fast as I can.

"Okay," Jordan says, and he takes my hand and leads me two lines over to his bus line.

If the other kids weren't staring before when they saw Jordan take my hand, they're definitely staring now. Especially the kids who wait in Jordan's bus line.

The girls dress like Kristin and the boys dress like Jordan does, and they all already have a tan because they went someplace tropical with their parents for Easter break, like Jordan did. Every year he goes to the Bahamas with his parents in the spring, and every year he comes back with a tan. None of the kids on the country club side of town have a watch tan line like Jordan, but that's because he's the only kid in the whole school who got a TAG Heuer for his eleventh birthday.

The longer we stand here, the littler I feel. My white

Chucks are a mess at this point. I wear boy Levi's, because my brother's clothes are the only ones that are long enough for my legs and narrow enough for my hips. I'm wearing a *Raiders of the Lost Ark* T-shirt that's a size too small, and a red bandanna for a belt.

Jordan feels me shrinking, but he doesn't know why, thank Christ (ten Hail Marys).

"We're going to find her," he whispers close to my ear. He takes my hand again and I feel a little bit bigger.

When we get to Jordan's house, he lets us in with his own key and then he runs to a beeping box on the wall and punches in a bunch of numbers. He's a latchkey kid like Kristin. I stay in the entryway because I'm pretty sure my destroyed Chucks are going to leave dirty prints across the spotless floor. Plus, I can hardly see straight with all the light.

There are windows on the walls, windows on the ceiling, and walls that *are* windows, and everything else in between seems to be made of glass or thick beams of wood. The rooms are huge. It's like every room is a frame for a photo waiting to happen, and beyond every window is the green forest.

"You live in a museum," I say, but not in a bad way, because it makes sense. Jordan's never had anything but beautiful stuff. No wonder everything he does is so . . . beautiful.

"Why are you standing in the doorway?" he asks.

"'Cause I'm scared to get anything dirty," I say, like it's obvious.

Jordan rolls his eyes and comes to take my hand and bring me into the kitchen.

"Are you hungry?" he asks.

"I'm always hungry," I tell him.

"Okay, but my mom's a snob. She doesn't buy chips or cakes from the grocery store," he warns.

"Neither does my mom," I say. Then I grin. "But it's because we can't afford them, not because we're snobby."

He laughs and takes berries and cheese out of the fridge. I eat the cheese, but the berries I leave alone, and of course Jordan notices.

"What's wrong with them?" he asks.

I shrug. "They've been in the fridge," I say.

He smiles and leans closer to me across the center island. "What's wrong with that?"

I make a face. "Jordan. I grew up picking berries off the vine and eating them warm from the sun." I point to the mummified things he's put in front of me. "Those suck."

He laughs again. "Snob."

I'm surprised for a second, and then I'm not. "I guess anyone can be a snob about anything," I say.

He nods. "And you *are* a snob."

I don't think he's being mean. He's got to be teasing. "Yeah, right," I say with a chuckle.

It's his turn to make a face. "Annie. Nothing's ever good enough for you."

I'm too stunned to say anything. I know people think Nora's a snob because she never joins in, but it's not for the reasons they think. Nora doesn't go to sleepover parties because she doesn't have a sleeping bag, and she doesn't laugh and joke around with the other kids because their jokes seem silly to her. And they are, considering how she's always just about to get killed by Fay or Bridget. I know how other people look at Nora. I just never thought anyone looked at me that way, too. But I guess they do. I want to tell Jordan he's got me all wrong, but I can't. Not unless I'm ready to tell him everything, which I never *ever* will.

"Are you finished?" Jordan asks after a while. I nod. "Then let's go," he says.

It's a great spring afternoon. Still a little chilly, but the sun when it hits you through the leaves is polka dots of warmth.

I tell Jordan about the Prue Tree and about finding Nora's circles in the dirt under it. I tell him about all the places we Bianchis like to go.

"But she'll have needed food," he says. "Where could she find something to eat?"

"There's the Lady Slipper Grove," I say with a gasp. "Maybe she went there. Lady slippers are a kind of orchid, and I'm pretty sure you can eat their bulbs."

"Show me," he says.

I lead Jordan through the woods. The broad-leaved oaks and maple trees give way to slender white birch trees the farther you go. And farther still are the hemlocks. Tucked deep between them and the black-spotted trunks of the birches is an open hollow where the sun comes down now that a big old tree has fallen. That's where the lady slippers are. They're snowy white and lovely. Jordan has this dreamy look on his face, and he starts to walk out into them, but I stop him.

"No, don't," I say, catching him by the arm. "They'll die. They're really fragile."

We look around, but it's obvious that no one's been digging up bulbs.

"Nora hasn't been here," he says.

He's right. The sun shines hot but the wind blows cold, and I know Nora's been out in this for days now and I can't find her.

"Where is she?" I ask, but it comes out a sob and then I'm crying. I've never cried in front of Jordan before because lab partners don't cry, not even when their experiments don't work.

I sit down on the ground and fold my arms over my head because I hate crying in front of Jordan and because I know I'm the only one who'll cry for Nora.

"Why did she run away?" Jordan asks. I never actually said to him that Nora ran away, but he knew anyways.

"Because no one cares," I say through my sobs.

"No one cares about Nora?" he asks.

"No one cares about anyone," I say.

I hear Jordan laugh, and I look up at him because now I'm angry that he laughed.

"How can you say no one cares about anyone?" he says. He looks sort of angry, but it's like he's hurt, too. "I care about you, don't I?"

I've dragged him out into the middle of a forest when he should be at baseball practice, so I know that he's not lying. And not just about this, because there have been about a thousand times Jordan's done stuff that nobody else would do for me, but even still. He's only like that with me because he doesn't know the whole story. If he knew the whole story, he'd run faster than Nora.

"No one cares about Nora except me. And I'm not enough for her to stay," I say. "I wish I was, but I'm not, and I never was, so she never even let me love her to begin with."

Jordan sits down on the ground next to me. "Then how can Nora run away because no one loves her?" he asks. "You do."

He just doesn't get it. He has no idea how terrible everyone was to Nora—or how terrible people can be to each other *period*, and I'm glad for that at least. I don't want Jordan to ever know.

I lean my head to the side and let it rest on his shoulder. "Yeah," I say. "I love her more than anything."

He leans his head against my head. "She'll come back," he promises.

"Maybe, but . . ." I think for a while about what it will be like now that she's actually run away. "I don't think she'll ever really come back."

We walk toward my side of the forest without talking, but after a while I start to worry that Jordan might want to walk all the way back to my house with me, and I tell him to turn around and go home because it's getting late. He shifts from foot to foot for a while, and I wait for him to spit it out, but he never does.

"If you don't want me to walk you home, at least be careful, okay? It's getting dark," he tells me, but not in a nice way. It's like he's growling at me or something.

I walk toward home with a frown, not sure what it

was I said that made Jordan so angry with me. Maybe it's something I didn't say. Maybe I should have said thank you. I'll do it tomorrow at school. I'll tell him thank you for skipping baseball when you love it so much and wandering around in the woods for four hours and not finding anything, and I should have said thank you a million times already and I don't know why I haven't yet.

I see the police cars parked in front of our house before I even make it out of the woods. I run the rest of the way and throw the front door open, scared they're going to tell me something awful.

Chapter Twelve

Nora's sitting at the kitchen table.

She looks like she's been crying, but otherwise she doesn't seem hurt. I let out a big sigh and practically collapse onto the pew. That's when I notice everyone else in the room.

There are two police officers, but neither of them is from Ashcroft. I have no idea where my parents are, but there's a woman sitting next to my sister with her mouth all pinched up, like she either disapproves of pretty much everything around her except for Nora, or she's afraid of it.

And it's like I see the kitchen as she sees it. I see our house as she sees it.

There's this thing I do to forget about it, even though I never really forget. I just look at the spot I'm in, and

I don't think too much about all the junk that's piled up around me. I don't think about the stacks of useless brochures that come in the mail even though Mom never orders anything from them. I don't think about the cans and jars and leftover boxes and the broken bicycles and the stacks of laundry or the bags and bags of other bags that my mother never *ever* throws away.

It's not like our house is full of garbage. It's not like dirty dishes are stacked everywhere and there are bugs. It's just that there's so much useless stuff everywhere you can hardly turn around without knocking something over.

There are paths through the stuff that my feet know so well I don't even have to look at all the junk anymore. I ignore it. I pretend it isn't there. You get used to it because you have to. Because you don't have any choice but to pretend, pretend, pretend. We've all been pretending for so long now it took someone walking in and seeing this place to make us remember that this isn't normal. This isn't the way other people live.

It's not like we're all crazy—I mean, we *know* it's bad. That's why we never bring anyone home, but we just look past it. And every year we try to clean it up. I ask my mother where to put stuff, and she tells me to put it in another room. The stuff never goes anywhere; it just gets shifted so we can clean under it. And if you do get rid of stuff, like expired cans of beans no one even knew were at the back of the cabinet because all these pots and pans are in front of them, then Mom just goes and brings home more things to pile around herself.

Walls and walls of junk. Mazes of useless stuff, when all of us need things we don't have. We don't have enough, so Mom never lets go of anything, because what if she needs it one day and doesn't have it? That's the thing, you see. It's not that my mom's dirty, or lazy, or any of the things you might think when you walk in the front door of 17 Snow Lane. My mom never stops cleaning, never stops working. Never stops trying. It's just that she's scared. And the stuff makes her feel protected.

But how do you explain that to someone who's sitting at your table and looking at you like this woman is looking at all of us right now? It's too real. It's too in-your-face, all this stuff. The beatings happen and then they're over and you can play them down to an outsider. You can call it a spanking or just a slap. This—the way this house is—you can't ignore it or play it down or explain it to someone else seeing it for the first time.

The beatings don't show how messed up we are, but our house does. 17 Snow Lane gives us away. And I see that now, looking at this woman sitting next to Nora looking around at how messed up we are, and I finally *see* it. I see it all now. The junk. The chaos. The crazy.

And in a way, I can't believe I didn't see it before. But you do what you have to do, don't you? You tell yourself what you have to tell yourself to hold on to whatever it is that's outside of all this insanity that makes you feel normal. So you never tell your friends and you never let them inside and you pretend that you're as normal as they are, because you just wouldn't be able to get through the day if you didn't.

But it's not normal. And it's not okay. And I see that now and I can't stop seeing it.

Now what am I going to do?

The woman sitting next to Nora forces her lips into a smile. "You're Annie, right?" she asks.

I nod.

"Your parents didn't know where you were," she says. "Can you tell us where you've been all afternoon?"

I don't say anything, because what can I say? There's nothing I can say that will make any of this better.

"Does that happen a lot?" she goes on. "Do you go away and not tell anyone? Does anyone ask where you've been?"

I shrug.

"You know that's not the way other families do things, right?" she asks.

"Who are you?" I ask.

She smiles really big. "I'm Miss Rastin, Annie. I'm a social worker, and I'm here to help you."

The social worker talks to each of us alone. I go upstairs while she talks to my sisters and my brother and I sit on the roof so nobody stares at me. The thing about being the youngest of nine kids is that you're never alone, but you're always lonely. Like this homeless person I saw taking a bath on the street in Dorchester once. No one will help you, but everyone's watching, and you have to do your most private stuff right out in the open.

When it's my turn, I go back downstairs. Fay is just leaving the playroom, and she and Miss Rastin are smiling and talking to each other like they're best friends. I wonder what's in this for Fay, because she never smiles like that unless she thinks she can get something for it.

"Come in and sit down, Annie," Miss Rastin says. I do, and she closes this little notebook she has in her hands. "I'm sure this is hard for you," she says.

"I'm just glad Nora's home," I say. "That's where I was this afternoon, you know. Looking for her in the woods. And my parents usually know where I am, even if they don't know for sure. I mean, I'm always in one or two places."

Miss Rastin nods and smiles with her mouth closed.

"Mm-hmm," she says. "Do you feel like you have to defend your parents a lot? Or make excuses for the things they did or didn't do?"

Oh Jesus (fifteen Hail Marys). She's right, but she couldn't be more wrong at the same time.

"So, Annie. I hear you're really popular at school," she says.

"I am?" I ask, and Miss Rastin laughs.

"Nora tells me you have lots of friends and everyone likes you."

I shrug. "I got lucky," I say, thinking of Kristin, and Sarah, and Karen, and even Samantha, who can be tricky sometimes, but at least she's honest. And, of course, Jordan.

"Do your friends come over after school a lot?" she asks, but she knows the answer. I stare at her. "Annie, I understand why you don't want to talk to me."

I raise one eyebrow. It's enough. She laughs again and looks me over for a long time.

"I heard you were funny, and I understand that, too. Humor is a great way to deflect feelings. Making people laugh is great, but it doesn't really make anything better. You know that, don't you?"

Okay. She's got me there.

"Yes," I say, looking down. She's not an idiot, but that doesn't mean I trust her. I look back up at her.

"Why are you asking us each questions alone? Are we all in trouble because Nora ran away?"

She shakes her head and opens her notes. "I don't want you to feel pressured by anyone else in the family to say one thing or another."

"So if I'm not in trouble, I can go, right?"

She smiles, but not in a happy way. "The State of Massachusetts is trying to determine if you're safe. Do you feel safe, Annie?"

This woman has no idea what she's talking about. Of course I'm not safe. I've never been safe.

"We found your sister Eleanor in Connecticut, riding the buses. She exploited a loophole in the ticketing system and was living on one of the bus lines for days. Do you know why we brought Nora back?" she asks. I shake my head. "She said she had to come back for her little sister. She said she couldn't leave you here with no one to take care of you." I nod because that sounds like Nora. Miss Rastin continues, "Is it true? Is there no one to take care of you?"

"They all take care of me," I say. I think of Fay and feel like I should add to that answer. "In different ways. It's a group effort."

The social worker narrows her eyes at me. "You're smart, Annie. You're tough. And you don't have to do this anymore if you don't want to."

There are lots of times in my life when I feel like I have no idea what people are talking about. It happens all the time when I'm around the girls at school, because all they have to think about are boys and stickers and sleepover parties, and I never have time to think about those things. The strange thing is, I know exactly what this woman is talking about, and there's no way in hell I'm going to admit to anything, because I also know she wants to take me away from my family.

"We know about the abuse, and that alone is enough to warrant placing you in a foster home."

I stand up to run, but stop myself before I actually bolt for the woods because I can see the cop from another town standing on the back steps. I sit down. I look at Miss Rastin and she looks at me. I guess I'd be sad if I didn't feel so cornered.

"Is Nora leaving?" I ask.

"Not without you," she tells me.

"Well, Jesus, Mary, and Joseph," I say, and I just don't care how many Hail Marys that is. I'm done saying Hail Marys. I'm done counting. "What the hell am I supposed to do with that?"

"Anything you want." She leans toward me, and I think this is the first time I've seen her real face. "You don't have to stay here and cover up for them anymore. You can start over."

I realize Miss Rastin is wicked young. She's, like, barely older than Miriam. She's got nice clothes on, too. Maybe she's from a rich family and she's smart, so she probably went to a good school. She's studied a lot. She's a social worker, so she's doing this because she wants to be a good person, and maybe she is. But she has no idea what she's talking about, because I love my family. I love my family as much as she probably loves hers, but I bet she doesn't know that. I bet anyone who looked at our family from the outside would think it was this huge act of kindness to take me away from it. Maybe for Nora that's true, but not for me.

"So who will I be if I start over?" I ask her.

"Anyone you want."

"Just not me."

She leans back and works really hard not to look emotional anymore. She stands up. "I was hoping for more from you, Annie."

"More what?" I ask, standing up with her. I'm angry now. "What am I supposed to be?" I laugh and change my voice, because it's all a joke now. "What's my destiny, Carl Sagan?"

She folds up her notes and gestures to the door like I've been dismissed. "Annie, I just want you to know that *this*"—she spins her finger around the room to include the whole house—"ends when you want it to end."

I don't leave the room. In a few minutes they're going to tell me to pack and say good-bye. And then I'm going to go to some stranger's house in another town and my whole life will be social workers and borrowed moms who don't hit me or love me.

"So you're telling me to run away, like Nora?" I ask. "You said she was riding around in circles when you found her. Is that what I'm supposed to do from now on?"

Miss Rastin really looks at me, and I feel like she's not trying to win anything anymore. She sits down.

"Okay, Annie. What do *you* want to do?" she asks me.

I think about this for a long time, because it's only the second time someone's ever asked me that. Well, okay, maybe not exactly, but at the beginning of the school year Mrs. Weiss asked me what my destiny was, and that's basically the same thing. Both of them are about me deciding for myself what my future is going to be like, and I'm finally ready. I finally have an answer to Mrs. Weiss's question.

"I want to make it better. And not just for us kids, but for Mom and Dad, too. I want it to be us, but not the worst us. I want the best us. Even if that's still a little crappy."

Miss Rastin laughs again.

"But we need help," I say, and I feel like crying all of a sudden, because I can't believe how hard it is to ask for this. And what a relief, too. It's a huge relief to just admit I can't do this alone. "I need help."

Miss Rastin's face softens. She swallows hard and lets me hear her real voice again, not her social worker voice.

"Okay, Annie," she says. "I'll think about how to help you, and I'll do my best. But that's *if* everybody in your family wants to do the work, too, and I gotta tell you, that's a big *if*. I can't promise you anything."

I smile at her for real, because she's stuck with me and I'm stuck with her, but at least we're going to try.

My parents are allowed "contact with the endangered children" again and the cops let them out of their bedroom so they can join the rest of us in the kitchen. After the cops and the social worker leave, Miri comes home. So we're all here. There's plenty of yelling. And crying. And people telling each other how sick to death they are of this family. Half of us think therapy might work, and the other half just space out and stare at the walls, wishing they were anywhere but here.

Yup. My family staying together is a big, fat IF.

Chapter Thirteen

Miss Rastin comes to see me every Tuesday and Friday at school.

We walk around the soccer field and talk all through free period at the end of the day. Most of the time, talking about my family problems with Miss Rastin feels like how my mom cleans. Piles of stuff get moved from one room to another so you can scrub under them a little, but none of the junk ever gets thrown out. But sometimes she really shows me something I didn't even know was there. Like with my counting. She explained to me how that was just a way I kept my brain busy and quiet so I didn't have to face the truth. She said my whole family lived in denial, and my counting was how I dealt with the fact that no one was talking about the abuse.

We talk a lot about denial. It's tough to explain once

you've made it through to the other side of it, but I imagine denial is like a Jedi mind trick. Except it's your mind that's doing it to you, and instead of saying, "These aren't the droids you're looking for," denial waves a hand and says, "There is no mess here and that beating never happened," and the rest of you goes on about your day like it's the truth. Only it isn't. And pulling a Jedi mind trick on yourself has some pretty serious side effects. One's called post-traumatic stress disorder.

Miss Rastin told me I have it, but that I can work through it now because I'm not repressing my emotions anymore. I told her I've stopped counting, and she said it was because I'd stopped living in denial and I've accepted that I'm an abused child. I don't know if that's totally true or not, because I always thought abused children were starving and in the hospital or something, and I was never like that.

Miss Rastin also said my mom needs as much help as us kids do. But that's something I've always known. In a lot of ways, I think my mom is the one who needs help most of all. Now I'm just worried that she won't really get it, because you have to ask for help for it to work. I don't know if my mom has ever really asked—she sort of got pushed into it when Nora ran away and got caught by child services. Now Mom has to be in therapy or they're going to take Nora and me away. We'll see what happens. I want Mom to get better, but I don't know. The house got cleaned up right after all this stuff started happening, but I can already see her starting to make those piles again. It worries me.

But the hitting has stopped. Fay isn't torturing Nora anymore, but they still hate each other. Mom apologized. I forgave her and said that I never really blamed her in the first place because I never did. It was never *her*. I hugged her and she hugged me back and *that* was her, or at least who she always meant to be. She smells so good. Powder and lemons.

Another good thing is Miriam came home. Well, she sort of came home. She goes to group therapy with the rest of my family now. She'll never really come home again, I know that, but she's trying, so I consider that to be a good thing. If there's one thing I've always known being the youngest Bianchi, it's that you've got to take what good you can.

Miss Rastin says that we've only been doing this therapy thing for a month now, and it's going to take much longer than that to make real progress. When I asked how long, she sort of smiled at the ground and changed the subject, so I'll probably be in therapy for a long time.

Today's the last day of school, and when I ask Miss Rastin where we'll meet next Tuesday, she tells me that we won't. It's been decided that Nora and I are no longer "in crisis" and we can shift to group therapy on Wednesday nights with my whole family now.

I try to picture one therapist listening to all of my family's problems at the same time and I laugh. It'll be a zoo.

When our time's nearly up, I realize that this is it for Miss Rastin and me.

"You're a good person," I tell her. "Take care of yourself."

She laughs and shakes her head at me. "You know, Annie, I'm not worried about you. You're going to do Great Things."

I know her well enough now to hear her punctuation. Why do people talk to me in capital letters?

She walks me back inside early so I can say good-bye to all my friends before summer starts. It doesn't really bother me that everyone knows I have a social worker. No one treats me any differently than they did before, and I think that's on account of Kristin and Jordan. Kristin includes me in everything the girls do, and she won't let anyone say a bad word about me, and Jordan . . . well, he takes care of the boys. Not sure how he does that, because he told me not to worry about it.

I'm going to miss school mostly because summer is never a break for me. But I like the last day of school because of how happy everyone is and how nice they are to each other. Everybody really notices each other and they say they'll miss each other and it makes me wish this were the way it was all the time.

Jordan smiles when he sees me come back with Miss Rastin, and he walks me to my bus line.

"What's the matter?" he asks me when he notices how quiet I am.

"Just thinking about my destiny," I say.

"Did you figure yours out?" he asks.

"Not yet," I say. "But I'm thinking about it."

"Me too," Jordan says. "But I guess that was Mrs. Weiss's point. I guess she just wanted us to start thinking about it."

"Maybe you're right." I smile because he just made me feel so much better.

Jordan's quiet for a while, but in a thinking way and not in a clammed-up way. "Come to my baseball game tonight," he says.

"Yeah, I like baseball," I say. Then I remember. "But it's Friday. I may have to go on a date with one of my sisters."

Jordan gives me this totally horrified look, and I laugh. "Not on a date with my sister, but on my sister's date with her." I explain the rules for dating a Bianchi girl. When I'm done, Jordan frowns.

"You're the youngest, right?" he asks. I nod and he says, "So what are your parents going to do when *you* start going on dates?"

I think of all those guys trying to feel up my sisters, Stan being the first to come to mind, and almost gag.

"Why would I ever want to go on a date?" I say. "Especially since if I do get a weekend night off one of these days, I'd much rather spend it with you."

Jordan looks confused for a second, and then he rolls his eyes and smiles. "Good," he says, but I don't get what's so funny to him.

"Call me when you find out if you're coming," Jordan says right before we head in different directions.

"I don't have your number," I say. He gives it to me, and I have no need to add all the numbers together to find out if they are divisible by three. I think about it, but I don't need to do it the way I used to. I don't know, Miss Rastin. I'd call that real progress.

"Do you want me to write it down?" he asks.

"I can remember seven digits, Jordan. Especially since the first three are exactly like mine."

He smiles. "What's your number?" he asks. I tell him.

We stand there for a second, eyeing each other. I

wait, then let the other shoe drop: "Do you want me to write it down?"

He shakes his head like I'm driving him crazy and turns away to go to his bus line. We've both gone about three steps when he turns back around and says, "You can call me whenever, you know. All summer. You can call me whenever you want. Like, when you get home from the farm and stuff."

I shift from foot to foot. "But what if your parents answer?" I ask.

"Why would my parents answer my phone?" he asks.

It takes me way too long to figure it out. "You have your *own phone*?" I blurt out. "Like, your own *line* and everything?"

"Yeah. In my bedroom," Jordan says with a shrug.

It's like WrestleMania in my house every night to see who gets to use the phone first. I can't even imagine what it would be like to make a phone call without an egg timer in my face and an angry sister standing in front of me with a hand on her hip.

I notice Jordan looks serious again. "Annie? Why would it matter if my parents answered?"

"Because they don't like me."

He looks away. "It's not you. They don't know you,"

he says quietly. "Just call me later, okay? I don't want to spend half the night looking up into the stands to check if you're there or not."

"I will," I say. I realize I mean it. "Hey, Jordan?"

"Yeah?"

"Thanks."

He looks confused. "For what?"

I start to remember all the things I should be saying thank you for to him, and what comes out of my mouth is pretty much the lamest one. But it's also the easiest to say.

"For helping me look for my sister."

"That was a month ago," he says, like he can't believe I'm bringing this up right now.

"Well, I figured it took me two months to apologize for embarrassing you in the cafeteria, and it only took me one month to say thank you for being a good friend, so it's like I'm getting better at this, right?"

Jordan looks at me for a while. "You're welcome," he says. And then we walk to the buses that take us to different sides of the woods.

Nora is already waiting on our bus. The ride home is quiet. As the bus stops in front of our house and Nora and I get off, I can see that the front door's open. Halfway across the lawn I can hear my brother, JP, talking in the kitchen. He says something that makes everyone laugh.

Nora and I stand outside 17 Snow Lane. I look at her and smile, and she smiles back at me. I don't know what my destiny is. I don't know if my family is going to make it or not. But we're going to try.

Acknowledgments

I have to thank Liz Szabla and Jean Feiwel at Feiwel and Friends for guiding me and getting this book in shape. It's hard for any writer to see the forest when she's in the trees, doubly so if she's lived in the trees her whole life. There is a certain amount of existential angst that goes along with telling a story partially based on your own childhood. When asked tough questions like, "What's the point of that?" it makes you stop and wonder what *was* the point of that major milestone in my development? Not a comfortable place to be, and Liz and Jean edited me ever so gently and wisely.

My writing lives on top of two rocks—my husband, Albert Leon, and my agent, Mollie Glick. They hold me up so I can pour myself out.

Finally, I thank my family. We have all been each other's heroes and each other's villains. We've saved each other and abandoned each other countless times. We've done our best and our worst either to, or in front of, each other. And all of it, good and bad, hilarious and downright ugly, has left me with enormous gratitude that you are mine.